It Is What It Is

A novella

Peter Wick

For Craig Joyce

("Milkbones all around")

Cover design by Ross Denyer.

Cover drawing by Peter Wick.

Special Thanks:

I also want to thank Joshua Malkin for meeting me for breakfast.

It Is What It Is
Chapter One

Four In the Morning

"Zenny!"

"Zenny! Wake up!"

"Zenny!"

They were yelling through the bedroom door, knocking loudly.

I held my head under the covers for a half-minute.

The dream had been killed.

I was climbing, climbing out of a big pit. It wasn't exactly a pit. I mean nothing in a dream - a good dream, anyway - is exactly the thing it is supposed to be.

It was more or less a pit, and I was climbing out of it, chasing a beautiful girl who was running off with my drum sticks. As she reached the top of a rock, she turned into an angel and spread her wings, holding my drum sticks far out of my reach.

The dream was killed.

Stella and Andre were still yelling through the door

"Zenny!"

"Zenny, IQ's missing."

"Zenny!"

Hm? IQ's missing? Again?

I sat up and looked emptily into the dark room.

I stood up and moved toward the light switch, stubbing my toe on a chair leg and stumbling awkwardly into the darkness. I avoided a blind face-plant, just catching myself on the back of a chair.

I hit the light switch and opened the door.

"Something's happened. I'm worried," Stella blurted.

Andre was calmer. "He disappeared."

I blinked awkwardly at them.

"It's like last time," Stella said. "He tossed his wallet. His phone's off. Probably tossed it in the street."

I understood their concern. Something bad has happened. And this isn't the first time IQ's done this.

"After everything that's happened…" Stella trailed off.

I just stood there staring at the two of them. Maybe it was the unsettled feeling I had from the dream being killed off. I don't know why, but I couldn't speak.

The Band

I am more or less in love with Stella. Normal people consider her too young for me.

She's 24.

She's beautiful in a rock and roll girl sort of way. You know, she doesn't spend too much time trying to look perfect. On her best day she doesn't give a shit what you think of her. She has a take-no-prisoners attitude on stage that sort of kills me.

I'm 49.

You don't remember the band I was in, and no one remembers the drummer. It's okay.

I played drums for Gupper Fish. We made enough money from our first album, seventeen years ago, that I was able to buy this house.

Our second album, "Sink Like A Stone," did just that. It sank down the charts so fast I thought we would have to send money back to our fans.

Three months later we didn't have fans anymore, so we broke up.

Why didn't I spend all my money on drugs, booze, and women?

Hell, I don't know.

Maybe I knew it was the only time in my life I would ever make any money.

So I have this house.

My idea back then was to rent out space in the house to UCLA students - I'm a half mile from campus - but eventually 'students' turned into Stella and her band, and eventually they stopped paying rent. I can't kick them out, though. They've become family.

So far I haven't had the heart to tell them I'm running out of money. The moment will present itself sometime. The moment might even present itself before my money-apocalypse arrives.

But wait.

What the hell is going on with IQ?

I didn't remember going outside, but there we all were; myself. Stella, Andre, and GQ, IQ's brother. It was a joke on the magazine that he was called GQ. He had only worn torn up jeans and old t-shirts, exclusively, his whole life. He's the bass player.

Stella and Andre were arguing about whether to take the van or the Honda Civic, when the unmistakable piercing sound of a siren tore into the night.

The police car turned onto our street, pulled up to the curb and stopped. Two cops emerged from opposite sides of the car.

"Which one of you put in the call?" asked the first officer, a stocky weight lifter with a pathetic half-grown mustache.

"I did," said Stella.

"What's going on?"

"Our drummer disappeared. I have his wallet."
Stella showed the officer IQ's brown leather wallet. The officer took it and pulled out the I.D.

"Isreal Quay," he read.

"We call him IQ," said Andre.

The officer looked dismissively at Andre and asked, "How do you come to have his wallet?"

"It was just there on the sidewalk," Stella said. "We were at this club. He went outside to have a cigarette. Then he was gone. His wallet was there in the bushes."

The two officers looked at each other.

The weight lifter turned back to Stella. "You folks been drinking a little tonight?"

That set me off a little bit. "Look, man," I said, "someone's missing. Don't you think you should be asking about that, instead of accusing people of shit?"

The officer turned to me. He looked amused. "Alright," he said, "what can you tell me about this disappearance?"

"Well...man...nothing."

The officers looked at each other again and smiled.

Dog Dreams

I was back in bed. I didn't understand why.

The dog - a medium-sized German Shepherd - was sleeping at my feet. He was moving his paws the way dogs do when they dream.

It was a running motion but the legs weren't joining in, just a half-move of the feet.

He was making noises in his throat, like a low half-growl dream-bark.

The dog was dreaming he was the King.

He swaggered through the door and down the hall of his dog-castle, wearing a regal red robe with a gold belt. A crown sat loosely on his head.

"What's going on here?" he barked.

Two Dobermans held a cat between them in chains.

The cat's hind feet were held by restraints.
The cat yowled desperately as King Dog approached. King Dog walked right up to the cat and sniffed disapprovingly.

The cat became silent. It looked pleadingly at King Dog.

King Dog rolled his eyes and barked, "Off with her head," waving his paw dismissively. He turned away and disappeared behind the grand double doors to the King's chamber.

The cat's yowling wail faded as the double doors closed.

And then….oh crap!

Stella was shaking me awake in the back seat of the Civic. We had arrived at the police station.

"Zenny, Zenny, wake up."

"Oh god." I sat up and rubbed my eyes. "Don't you know how bad it is to wake someone up in the middle of a dream?"

"Come on, we have to go inside."

I stood awkwardly, barely able to focus. "My dog was dreaming this one."

"Hm?" Stella was trying to comb my hair with her hand.

"My dog was having this amazing dream."

"Zenny," she stopped combing my hair and held my face gently in her hands. "Zenny, you don't have a dog."

I blinked at her and shook my head a little.

"Come on," she said, and led me toward a pair of glass doors.

Last Night

"I need each of you to make a statement," the cop said. "Tell me everything you were doing, what your missing drummer was doing. Details. Give me details." He sat down opposite us in a plain black chair. "Let's start with you," he said, looking at me.

I looked over at Stella, coughed a couple times, and finally said, "No, man, um, I..I don't know anything. I wasn't there."

The officer's eyes tried to cut a hole in me.

"So, why are you here, exactly?" he asked.

"Well, I guess I was going to help look for the guy, you know. I mean IQ's missing. I'm here to help find him."

"Zenny owns the house we live in," Stella said.

"Zenny?" the cop asked.

"That's my name," I said.

"Zenny, is that short for something?"

"No, no, it's actually long….for 'Zen'," I said.

"Can I see your I.D. please?"

I reached for my pocket, but in the hurry and chaos I had left my wallet at home.

"I…I don't have my I.D."

The cop tapped his pen nervously on the arm of his chair.

"You don't have your I.D.?"

"Look, man, it was all happening so fast. I mean, I was asleep. They woke me up. We were outside. How about if we just get on with looking for IQ?"

The cop shook his head and sighed heavily. "Okay," he said, turning to Stella, "were you actually there? Can you make a real statement, with events that actually happened, that maybe you saw with your own eyes?"

"I can," Stella said.

The problem with listening to Stella is that I forget to actually listen to her. I look at the shocking streak of orange hair that invades her natural black. Her words and her voice wash over me like water.

Everyone knows she is going to be a star, a superstar, one of these days. It just hasn't happened yet.

When she puts that guitar over her shoulder and steps up to the mic, Andre, IQ, and GQ behind her, then she pounds out that first chord, leans to the mic, and belts out her unique gut-level, attitude-infused voice, colored with just a touch of sensitivity, well, I don't have words to describe how I feel.

I have to shake myself out of my trance, and remind myself to pay attention to what she's saying.

The story she told the cop didn't seem to satisfy him.

They had gone to the club to watch three different bands play. The first two bands rocked pretty hard, she said. The cop didn't care, but Stella had to comment on the show.

She was at the front of the crowd, with IQ by her side, for the second band's set.

As the set ended, Stella and IQ joined Andre and GQ in the bar. Andre was trying to pick up some girl who Stella thought was a little too trashy for him.

"She was a smart girl." Andre argued.

"Look," said the cop angrily, "can we just get through what happened? The events leading up to the disappearance?"

Stella continued.

The four of them hung out in the bar while the third band took the stage. None of them really liked the guys in the third band. They'd met them before and thought they were all pretentious assholes.

So they stayed in the bar while the pretentious assholes (not their actual band name, but it might as well be) played a bunch of lame pretentious asshole music.

A few friends of Stella's found her and the guys in the bar. It was an awkward moment, Stella explained, because she and IQ were having an argument.

After the pretentious assholes quit playing, no one was in a hurry to leave.

Except IQ.

"We were fighting," Stella said.

The cop cleared his throat and looked up from the paper he was writing on. "Are you and the missing party, um, involved?"

"That's kind of what we were arguing about," Stella answered.

There was tension in the room, and Stella was avoiding eye contact with Andre.

Andre stared at her with a sort of pissy expression.

"IQ and I had slept together," she said. There was a stony silence. "He wanted us to be together."

"And you didn't?" the cop asked.

"I told him I needed to figure some things out. He was really upset. He started acting like he did last time."

"Last time?"

Stella glanced at me, then Andre, then GQ. "He disappeared once before, six months ago. We found him crashing at some disgusting house, not eating, wasting away."

"Does the missing person have a history of drug abuse?"

Stella looked at the cop sideways. "He's searching for something," she said. "He says weird things sometimes. He's searching for something transcendent."

"What the hell is that supposed to mean?"

"I'm not sure," Stella said, quietly. "I don't think he knows either."

"Okay, let's get back to the events of last night. You argued. Then what?"

After the argument, IQ went outside to have a cigarette. When Stella, GQ, and Andre went out to find him he wasn't there. The sidewalk was empty.

All they found was IQ's wallet lying in the bushes.

The cop looked at the wallet. There was money inside; eighteen dollars.

The cop shook his head. "I assume you tried calling him, texting."

"His phone's off," Stella said. "Straight to voicemail."

"How is it," the cop asked, looking at me, "that we have I.D. for the guy who's missing, but you're sitting here and we don't have any I.D. for you?"

"Well, man," I said, "life is full of fucking irony.

Chapter Two

Summit Meeting

I was running up a hill.

It wasn't really a hill. Well, sometimes it was. sometimes it was the up-slope of a sound wave.

I was running after IQ. He was ahead of me. Sometimes he was so far ahead of me I could barely see him. Once or twice I got close enough to him I could almost reach out and grab him. Almost.

So I was chasing him, and then all of a sudden drum sticks were flying at us.

Dozens of drum sticks flying out of the forest like arrows.

I was scared.

I barely ducked in time to avoid being hit by an arrow-drum-stick.

Then IQ went down.

"Aaaaah!" he groaned, a drum stick sticking out of his heart.

Just as I was reaching out to help him, Stella was shaking me awake again.

"God dammit!" I growled sleepily.

"Sorry," she said.

"You keep waking me up in the middle of dreams. It's really messing with my head."

"It's just a dream," she said calmly.

"The first time it was just a dream. Now it's like an interruption in the flow of the cosmos. IQ was stabbed."

"What?" Stella's eyes widened. "What do you mean IQ was stabbed?"

"In my dream. Drum sticks were coming at us like arrows. One got IQ in the heart. I was trying to help him, but you woke me up."

It was about noon now. We had made it back from the police station around 7am.

I'd gone back to sleep.

Now I was scratching my head, trying to imagine a happy ending to the dream. That image of the drumstick arrow sticking out of IQ's heart bothered me.

"Come on," Stella said. "We're having a summit meeting."

"A summit meeting. That sounds heavy."

I sat up on the edge of the bed and, for the third time in less than eight hours, was blinking myself to full consciousness, or trying to.

I needed an hour of Zenny-med.

I don't know if it's actual meditation. I've never been trained in any kind of real meditation. I've kind of just made up my own version. I call it, "Zenny-med." I don't know anything about real Zen.

I've started to depend on my made up half-ass Zenny-med. Once every day I try to sit on the floor and, well, and nothing. I just sit. That's as much as I can explain.

Thoughts come. Thoughts go. I don't control anything. I just sit and let whatever comes come.

After about an hour I get up and go do something. Or do nothing. Or maybe have a beer.

I need this hour of nothing.

Today was working against me.

I stood up and walked to the kitchen where Andre, GQ, and Stella were waiting for me. GQ was eating breakfast cereal dry out of the box.

"Morning," I said, to no one or to all of them. I opened the fridge looking for string cheese sticks.

"Okay," Stella said, "what are our options?"

I turned from the fridge and took a bite of mozzarella. The four of us stared at each other.

GQ shoved a handful of cereal into his mouth and said, "I guess I should call my parents in Santa Barbara."

"What are you going to tell them?" Stella asked.

"I don't know. I'll say he's missing again. The Police are looking for him. What else can I say?"

Andre cleared his throat. We all turned. "Remember the guy with the bandana?"

"Hm? What guy?" Stella took a sip from the cup in her hand and looked at Andre.

"At the show last night. He was in the bar. He went out to smoke with IQ. Last I saw, they were talking out there."

"Crooked nose," Stella said.

"Yeah, that guy. We should find him."

"Okay, that's a start," said Stella. That's something. But how do we find HIM?"

There was a hollow silence.

"And then there's the gig," Stella said.

Andre and GQ looked up. I had a sense that they were looking at me without really looking at me.

"What gig?" I asked.

"Tomorrow," Stella said. Glazer from Polymorph is coming."

I bit off a piece of mozzarella and looked from Stel a to Andre to GQ.

"Why's everyone looking at me?"

Stella locked her eyes onto me and walked up to me. "Look, this whole thing is shitty," she said. "I mean, IQ's probably gonna walk in the door as soon as I say this, but, Zenny, can you be our drummer for today? For tomorrow? If - I mean -" a half-tear welled up in her eye. "God, if he turns out to be okay, then I'm sorry for asking, but , but -"

"Sure," I said, "I can do the gig if he's not here, tomorrow."

"Thank you."

She reached her arms around me and hugged me I liked it.

"I don't want to be the reason you're not signed to Polymorph, though."

"Oh, stop," Stella said pulling out of the hug.

"You know, it's like Glazer watches the gig and says, 'nice band, but you gotta lose the crazy old drummer."

"Shut up," Stella said. "And anyway, Glazer's older than you are."

"When you have that much money, age counts different," I said.

"Zenny, shut up. You'll be awesome."

"So," Andre said. "How are we going to find bandana guy?"

"Max at the club," said Stella, eyes on her phone. She tapped a couple times and brought the phone to her ear. "Damn it! It's the fucking recording. Just tells you who's playing tonight. What's Max's cell number?" She looked up at Andre. "He lives there, upstairs in the club. He has a bed in, like, a big closet."

"How do you know where Max has a bed?" Andre asked.

"Please, Andre, this is no time to get pissy."

Andre looked a bit wounded.

"We have to go," Stella said. We have to go find Max, and see if he can tell us how to find crooked nose bandana guy."

There was a frozen silence.

Stella grabbed some keys and said, "Let's take the van."

She was halfway out the front door when GQ put his box of cereal down and followed her. I looked at Andre and bit off another piece of mozzarella.

"Hey, man," I said. "She knows where Max's bed is. What the fuck you gonna do?"

Andre didn't say anything. Finally he shook his head slightly and turned to leave.

I followed him out.

Chapter Three

Rusty

"Is there any chance we could practice?" I asked from the back of the van.

"Hm?"

"I mean, later today sometime. Tonight. Could we practice? This is an important gig, you know."

I didn't want to say what was really bothering me; I'm a little rusty. Plus, I only kinda know the band's songs.

"If we have time, Zenny," Stella said from the driver's seat. "We just have to do this first."

"Sure, I mean, of course," I said. "I mean, it's gonna be a great show no matter what. I was just thinking it would be better with a practice first."

"I agree," GQ said.

"I'm not arguing," said Stella. "Of course we want to practice. We just have to do this first.'

She turned onto Santa Monica Boulevard and headed out toward Los Feliz.

With The Lobster Allergies

She had parked the van next to the club and was standing looking up at a small window.

"Max!" she yelled. "Max!"

No answer.

Andre, GQ, and I were standing near the van trying not to look too awkward.

"Max!"

She reached down and picked up a medium sized pebble from the ground. She threw the pebble toward the window, missing by about six inches. It bounced quietly off the side paneling.

I reached down and picked up a small rock. I locked onto the window and threw.

The rock tapped the window and fell harmlessly back down to the ground.

"Max!"

A noise came from the window.

The window opened and a woman looked down at us. "Whaddyu want?"

"Is Max here?" Stella yelled up at her.

"Why do you want him?"

"We need to talk to him about last night."

"He's not here," the woman said.

"Can you give me his cell number?"

"Hell no."

"Shit!" Stella turned to me and sighed. Then she turned back to the woman.

"Where can we find him? It's important."

"He's with the Lobster Allergies."

"What?"

"The Lobster Allergies, the band."

"Oh, okay. Thanks."

The woman abruptly closed the window and disappeared.

"Fuck!" Stella shouted.

"The Lobster Allergies," I said. "I have -" I was scrolling through my contacts.

"Tommy, yeah. Their bass player."

I put my phone to my ear and waited.

"Hello."

"Tommy."

"Who's this?"

"Zenny."

"Who?"

"Zenny Zeller."

"Oh, hey man, what's up?"

I couldn't blame him. I hadn't talked to him in two years.

"Are you guys with Max?"

"He's in the other car. We're recording."

"Where? Where are you recording?"

"What's it about?" Tommy asked, suspicion creeping into his voice.

"Missing person," I said. "We're looking for a guy who went missing from his club last night."

"Shit, man," Tommy said. "Okay I'll get you his number."

"Where are you recording? We'll just be ten minutes. It would be easier if we could talk to him in person."

"Come up to Blake's. You know the house on stilts in the hills? It's off Laurel Canyon."

"Yeah, yeah," I said. "The recording studio in the fucking stilts house."

"That's the one," Tommy said.

"Cool. See you in a bit."

I hung up.

"Alright we can talk to Max," I said. "There's a recording studio in a crazy fucking house that gives me the creeps."

"You want to drive?" Stella was holding out the keys to the van.

I looked at the keys. "Okay," I said blandly. I didn't really want to drive. I always get lost in the hills. I also worry about driving off a cliff and killing everyone in the car.

I took the keys and sat behind the wheel. The others got in and I fired up the van.

Wrong turn

I got lost.

I missed a tiny little right turn off of the winding canyon roadway and, thinking it was the next turn, found myself facing the gate of a mansion with almost no room to turn around.

I backed up two feet, forward two feet, back, forward.

Two enormous and deadly dogs were barking murder at us from behind the gate.

Finally I got the van turned around, back out onto the winding canyon boulevard, and back to the right turn.

I found Blake's house and looked out at the view of Los Angeles. The sudden drop-off of the hill below us gave me a queasy feeling.

"Zenny."

Tommy was standing in the doorway of the house.

"Hey Tommy, How yu been?"

"Oh, you know, life's a bitch," he said. "Why you gotta go two years without talking to me? You hate me that much?" He was smiling as he said it.

"Yes," I said. "You're an asshole. Fuck you" We laughed together and gave each other a hug.

"You see Jimmy much these days?"

Jimmy was the singer-guitar player in "Gupper Fish."

"Hell no," I said. "He's too busy having a love affair with his own ego. And anyway he's back in Seattle."

"You're too hard on him," Tommy said.

I didn't really want to talk about Jimmy, so I walked into the house. Stella, GQ, and Andre followed me in.

"Zenny Zeller!"

It was Kafka, the singer. He'd gotten chubbier and lost his hair. Who was it who said, "Punk's not dead. It's just overweight, bald, and passed out on your couch"? They were probably talking about Kafka.

"Kafka, what's going on, man?"

"Recording some new songs."

"Cool, cool. Is anyone going to listen to them?"

"Of course man. Social fucking media. We have a lot of followers these days. We're tapping into the new generation."

"Yeah? That's exciting, for you and for your twelve followers."

"Fuck you, Zenny."

"Hey, where's Max?" I asked. "We don't want to take up too much of your precious time."

"Setting things up in the booth. I'll get him."

Kafka disappeared down a hallway, and everybody stood around awkwardly.

Tommy broke the awkwardness.

"Who are your friends, Zenny?"

"Oh, yeah, this is Stella, Andre, and GQ. Everyone this is Tommy."

"Hey,"

"Hi."

"Wazzup?"

"What's going on?"

"You all a band?" Tommy asked.

"Yeah," said Stella.

"What's your band? What do you call yourselves?"

"Stella," said Stella.

"What? Oh, you mean, you're Stella, and the band is Stella?"

"Yeah," she said.

"Hey, you all want a beer? Whiskey? Weed?"

I said no, even though a beer sounded pretty damn good. Stella shook her head.

Andre said no.

"Zenny, what the fuck kind of people you hanging out with?"

"I will," said GQ.

"Cool," Tommy said. "What'll it be?"

"Beer."

Tommy went into the kitchen as Max and Kafka came down the hall.

"Hey Stella. What's going on?" Max asked.

"Max! Thank god. Look, IQ disappeared last night."

"Disappeared, what do you mean?"

"From the club. One minute he was there, and the next minute he was gone."

"Shit," Max said. "What the fuck you want me to do about it?"

"We need to get in touch with that guy with the bandana, with the crooked nose. They were smoking together outside."

"Bandana...crooked nose...Oh shit, do you mean Johnny Blood?"

"Fucking Johnny Blood," Tommy said from across the room.

"Fuckin' Johnny Blood," said Kafka.

"Fuck man," I said. "I should'a known it was fuckin' Johnny Blood."

"What?" Stella said. "I don't know. Is that guy who wears the bandana?"

"That's the guy," said Kafka.

"Fuckin' Johnny Blood," said Tommy.

Fuckin' Johnny Blood

In every band there's always one member who is the problem member.

You never know who it's going to be.

The singer? Divas and egomaniacs.

The guitar player? Prima donnas always bitching that the bass player is dead weight, or that the singer gets too much credit.

In some bands it's the bass player, always complaining about indulgent guitar solos, and narcissistic celebrity musicians.

Once in a while the problem member is the drummer. Not often, though. Drummers are mostly pretty cool. We sit back and try our best to keep lame songs fun, pretentious songs simple...in my own humble opinion.

Johnny Blood plays guitar.

He was pretty good once, back in the day. Brilliant actually.

But Johnny Blood has been the problem member in more bands than I can count.

Early on he was the problem member because he was so damn good. He demanded too much from his bandmates. They couldn't deal with it.

Bands broke up.

Then he was the problem member because all the mind-altering substances he had used collected inside him until one day he achieved what he called "perma-high." He started sleeping crazy hours or he didn't sleep at all. He never showed up anywhere on time. He was only half-functional when he did show up.

Bands broke up - or kicked him out.

Later he was the problem member because he was just such an asshole all the time.

He was always starting new bands.

Max had given us an address. He wasn't sure if it was current, but Stella was back at the wheel driving us further east.

When we finally found the house it had all the tell-tale signs of fuckin' Johnny Blood living there.

Beer bottles - about twenty of them - lined the railing of the porch.

Vomit stained the front yard in three different places.

The front door was standing open, but no one appeared to be around.

I tapped on the door frame and said, "Hello."

Nothing.

We walked all the way in.

"Hello," shouted Stella.

"Fuck," said a female voice from a lump of blankets, clothing, and sort of a couch

An arm with a hand at the end of it pushed some blankets away, and a woman I recognized but hadn't seen in five years turned lazily toward us.

"Hi Verna," I said.

She looked at me and blinked. The years hadn't been kind to her. She looked like life had been dragging her through a cemetery feet-first.

"Who the fuck are you?" she asked.

"Zenny."

When she failed to respond to this, I dropped it and moved on.

"Where's Johnny?" I asked.

She slowly turned her body, throwing off the rest of the blanket and putting her feet on the floor.

She stood up. She was wearing only her underwear. It hung on her body like she hadn't eaten in a month. She stumbled away down the hallway.

I followed her

"Johnny!" she yelled through a door.

Sounds came from the other side of the door, resembling what you would expect to hear if someone scraped the strings of a violin with a pick-ax inside your head.

I realized it was the sound of an electric guitar that someone had fallen asleep on while it was still plugged in.

The door opened.

Fuckin' Johnny Blood, bald as a bowling ball without his bandana, stood in the doorway.

"Some jerk-offs are here looking for you," Verna said. "And get that bitch out of my house."

"Come on, Baby," said Johnny. "You should give us a chance. The three of us could have some fun together."

"If I ever see her again I'm calling the police."

"Baby," Johnny pleaded.

"These people are looking for you." Verna turned and walked past us, disappearing back into the living room.

Fuckin' Johnny Blood looked at me. "Hey, man," he said.

"Blood, what's up? Been a while."

"Yeah," he said absently. "Been a long fucking time. What's going on? Why you here?"

"We're looking for IQ," I said.

"Fuck. Who?"

"IQ. You were hanging out with him last night."

"Oh, IQ, Yeah, that guy."

He was rubbing his eyes, trying to massage some l fe back into his head.

"You went outside to have a cigarette with him," Stella said. "Then he was gone."

Johnny stared off at nothing for a moment.

"I was with him," Johnny said.

"Yes," Stella said. "We wondered if you knew where he went."

"No, I mean I went with him. We got into some limousine. Buncha fuckin rich kids. You know, Daddy runs Warner Brothers or some shit. They randomly stopped and told us to get in. We rode around with these fuckin' rich assholes."

Stella glanced toward me with a hopeful look.

"Oh man, "Johnny said. "That's was a wild night."

"Where did you go? What happened?"

"Went to some giant mansion in Malibu. Partied hard, man. Those fuckin' rich kids…"

"What about IQ?"

"I don't know," Johnny said. "Maybe he's still out there."

"In Malibu?"

"Maybe. I don't know."

Stella, Andre, GQ, and I all looked at each other.

"How did you get home?" Stella asked.

Johnny turned and looked toward the bed. "She drove me here."

I peeked around the corner of the doorframe. Stella peaked around with me.

Buried under blankets was the shape of a female body. Blond hair hung down the side of the mattress.

"Can we wake her up?" Stella asked. "We have to go check this place out."

"Sure," Johnny said. "Fuckin' wake her up. Take her with you. I don't fucking care."

Stella went to the bed and leaned down over the sleeping girl. She began shaking the girl awake. "Hey," she said gently. The blond hair moved and a face emerged. She was young - twenty, twenty-one at most.

Stella's face was inches from hers. They looked into each others eyes smiling for a moment.

Then the girl was suddenly lucid and sitting up. "What the fuck!" she said.

"It's alright," Stella said calmly. "We're here to-"

"Where the fuck am I?" she said.

"My house," said Johnny.

"Who the fuck are you? Oh, shit!" She put a hand to her head as the previous night began to clear through the fog of her memory.

Stella sat down next to her. "Don't worry. We're just here to try to find our missing drummer. He might have been with you last night. A mansion in Malibu?"

The girl was looking at her phone, then looked up at Stella. "What'd he look like?"

"Six feet tall. Short black hair. A week's worth of stubble."

"Maybe," the girl said. "What was he wearing?"

"Jeans. Plain white t-shirt."

"Yeah, I might have seen him," the girl said.

"Look," said Stella urgently, "we need to find him. Can we go to this house? Can you call someone, find out if he's still there?"

The girl already had her phone to her ear. She waited a few seconds.

"Hey...sorry...I don't know...some house...don't tell him....I don't know, tell him I went home...Fuck!....what!?...WHAT!? You WHAT!?....Fuck you, Gina...Bitch!....No, look...Gina, let me talk!...Fuck you and fuck him....Gina there's some fucking people

– I don't give a shit about that...Listen, there's some people here looking for a guy who might have been there with us last night....black hair, I don't know, can I just send them out there?...I don't care, can I just fucking send these people?...alright...I don't care...because you're a bitch and I'm never talking to you again...and that goes for him too...no...I'm not going to talk to him...goodbye....goodbye."

She hung up angrily.

"Fuck!"

We all stood still. I was trying not to smile too broadly at the awkwardness everyone felt.

She looked up. "The bitch slept with my boyfriend last night."

Johnny laughed. "Hey, what goes around comes around."

She didn't laugh. "He might have been there," she said. "Maybe still is. She said there's ten or fifteen people passed out downstairs."

Chapter Four

Earth Opens Up

I had a drink in my hand.

It was sort of a martini glass with some kind of purple liquor in it. It tasted like small bugs.

Bugs!

They were bugs. And it wasn't a martini glass at all anymore. I was holding a small bug colony, out of which climbed a guy I knew twenty years ago named Sloan. I don't remember his full name. I only knew him as Sloan.

But we didn't have time to say hi to each other because the ground was moving, opening up. The ground swallowed Sloan up, deep into a crevice.

The shaking stopped.

"Help!" Sloan shouted.

I could see him. "Hold on. I'll reach down. Grab my hand."

I braced myself against a rock and reached down into the crevice. Sloan reached up. Our hands were inches apart.

I shifted and lowered my hand another inch. He stretched his arm to bring his hand an inch closer. Now our fingertips were touching.

What's all that honking? What the fuck!

Goddamn it!

I woke up in the back seat of the van, as Stella yelled, "Let me in, asshole!"

We were surrounded by traffic, none of it moving, on the 101 freeway.

"Asshole!" Stella yelled again, and honked the horn.

I sat up.

My tongue was dry. My eyes didn't fully open. My face felt like it had been twisted sideways by the back of the van seat.

"Damn it," I muttered to myself.

"What?" Stella asked.

"Nothing," I said.

The van wasn't moving. All traffic surrounding us had stopped. Stella turned around.

"Sorry," she said.

Our eyes met. She knew.

She knew she had woken me up from another unfinished dream.

I smiled at her. "Just some asshole I knew twenty years ago, being swallowed up by the Earth."

She laughed. "Is he gonna get out?"

"Not now," I said solemnly.

"What the hell are you two talking about?" Andre asked, without ever opening his eyes?

Stella looked back at me, smiling. GQ was sitting in the passenger seat, in the front of the van. He was quiet, but that was normal for him. For some reason, though, it struck me as odd just how quiet he was being.

"Hey Stella," I said.

"Yeah?"

"Get out of this traffic. Let's get something to eat."

Stuck Up Prick

Forty minutes later we were finally sitting at a table in a cheap diner in North Hollywood.

It was five in the afternoon. Rush hour was in full hell mode.

The waitress took our orders, and we sat back, collecting our respective selves. We all looked across the table at each other.

"GQ, how's it going?" I asked.

He shrugged. He avoided making eye contact.

Andre began tapping his fingers on the table. "We should just go home and practice," he said. "Fuck IQ."

Stella glared at Andre. A stony silence fell on the table.

The waitress arrived with water glasses, soda, and Stella's salad. She turned and left. Stella picked up a fork and half-heartedly stabbed at some lettuce.

Andre's eyes met mine and I quietly shook my head.

Andre opened his mouth to speak again. "What I'm - "

"Fuck IQ!?" Stella whispered angrily, checking behind her to make sure no one was eaves-dropping. "Fuck you, Andre, for saying fuck IQ. And fuck you for being so smug and pissy all the time. All the fucking time."

"Are we going to do this now?" Andre asked, in a smug and pissy tone of voice. "Fine, let's go."

"Look, you're a brilliant musician. You know that," Stella began, still barely louder than a whisper. "That's why I put up with your bullshit. You're brilliant. But, Andre, sometimes you can be a real stuck up prick."

"Okay," Andre replied calmly. "Which of us is the real backbone of the sound that defines this band? Is it you, strutting around like a goddamn peacock? Or is it the musical atmosphere that backs you up and carries you into the offices of fucking Glazer from Polymorph? Shall we take a vote?" Andre looked at me smugly.

"Don't look at me," I said. "I vote half Stella and half the guy we're looking for."

"IQ? Are you serious?"

"Don't knock drummers, man. All the old jazz guys used to say the drum is the most important instrument. There are things IQ does behind you that are so subtle you don't even know he's doing them. That's why I'm a little nervous about taking his place tomorrow night."

"You, of all people, should be on my side," Andre said.

"Oh? Why's that?"

"I mean, look." Andre sat up in his seat and coughed.

The waitress arrived with our plates.

There was an awkward pause while the waitress put plates in front of each of us. Then she stood and asked the routine question, "Anything else I can get for you?"

"No."

"We're good."

"Thanks."

She left.

I picked up a fry, stabbed it into some ketchup, and looked at Andre. "You were saying?"

"Never mind," he said.

We began eating. I knew he couldn't stop himself, and I was right.

"Alright, look," he said. "You're a good drummer. You have a good style. I like jamming with you. That's why I'm okay with this idea." He waved his hand around the table to indicate the four of us as a band. "But you've got to admit you're this close to being a washed up has-been. This is your second chance. Fuck IQ. I like you on drums better than IQ, and if this doesn't happen for you, what's out there for you? How much longer is your money going to last?"

Stella was holding her head in her hands, looking down into her salad. GQ was leaning back, detached, slowly shoving fries into his mouth.

"About two months," I said.

Stella looked at me with a quizzical expression.

"What do you mean?" she asked.

"Two months," I said again. "That's about how long my money is going to last."

"What!? No, wait...WHAT!?"

"I didn't really want to tell you guys. It's not supposed to be your problem. A couple years ago I took out a loan on the house. That's really what we've all been living on. In a couple months I might have to start skipping payments. That goes on long enough, the bank takes the house away."

A frozen silence.

"Zenny! What the fuck!"

"Don't worry about it. It's not your problem."

"Yes it is," Stella said. "If it's your problem it's our problem. Especially since we live in your house."

"Okay, yeah," I said, "it, it kind of is your problem, too."

Andre made a gesture toward me. "So what are you planning to do?"

"I don't know, Andre. I hadn't exactly settled on a plan yet."

"So here's your plan," he said. "We get this deal with you as our drummer. We become rock stars. Your house is saved, and you get a second chance at your career. A feel-good story all the interviewers and bloggers will eat up."

I shook my head at him. "I'm not going to step on my good friend IQ just to save my own ass. There's some other solution."

Stella put a hand up. "Stop. Just stop," she said. "Zenny, he's not a better drummer than you. You two are both great. Andre, I'm not going to argue with you. I don't feel like doing this right now. If you want to go home, you find your own way home. If you want to ride in the van, the van is going to Malibu to look for IQ. That's all I have to say. Now I just want to eat."

I looked at Andre, smiled at him and shrugged. I picked up my burger and took a bite.

"Damn," I said. "This is pretty fucking good."

Daddy's At The Hampton's House

An icy silence filled the van.

It was an hour later and traffic was a little bit better - only a little bit.

We headed east for a while, without conversation.

Eventually Stella got off the freeway and we wound our way through Malibu Canyon.

She pulled off the road and punched something into her phone. She looked out at the road and continued driving.

A couple miles later she turned onto a small road that disappeared up a hill. We snaked our way up the hill and found ourselves facing an enormous double gate that might have been used as the model for the gate to heaven.

Stella stopped the van and made a call.

"Hi...is this Gina?...Sheri gave me your number...Mmhm, yeah, I'm Stella...we're at the gate...Okay, thanks."

She hung up and dropped her head into her hands. She rubbed her eyes and forehead.

The gate began to open.

We drove slowly up a grand curving driveway, with a classic-looking Roman fountain in the middle.

We parked in front of the most gigantic house - if 'house' is even the right word – I have ever seen, and I've seen a few.

A perky twenty-something girl was bounding down the steps toward us, as we all climbed out of the van.

"Hi."

"Hi," Stella said.

"So, you're friends with Sheri?"

"Well..." Stella looked at me. "No, not really."

Gina looked puzzled. I decided to try to help.

"We just met her today. She spent last night fucking an asshole I used to know."

"What the fuck."

"Hey, aren't you the chick who fucked her boyfriend?"

Maybe I wasn't helping, after all.

"Who the fuck are you guys?" she asked.

Stella gave me a quick look to stop me from talking. We're looking for a guy we think was here last night. Our drummer. He's missing."

Gina looked torn between helping us, and kicking us off the property.

"There were a lot of people here last night," she finally said.

"Is anyone left? Can we come in and look?"

"You can come look," Gina said. "But most of 'em are gone now."

We followed Gina up the steps and into a grand entranceway that belonged in some french castle before the people of France decided to chop the heads off all their royals.

"We had to have the party," Gina said, "since Daddy's away. He's at the house in the Hamptons, in New York." She spoke as she led us through the grand hallway to a stairway that led downstairs. "He never lets us throw parties when he's home, even though he has his own cocktail parties all the time."

"Who's your Daddy?" Stella asked, only slightly mockingly.

"Jack Anderson."

She paused, waiting for us to act impressed.

"He runs Sony Studios," she said.

"Oh, wow," I said, half-heartedly.

"That's awesome," said Stella, also with half-assed enthusiasm.

The stairway led down to something that was much more than a recreation room. It was bigger than most clubs the band had played at. It had a slightly different flavor from the grand opulence of the upstairs.

The most noticeable difference, though, was the presence of four half-naked bodies passed out on purple velvet couches that lined the room.

None of the four people were IQ.

Also lining the room were a handful of coffee table sized, well, coffee tables with mirrors for table tops, on top of which were the remnants of what must have been a crap load of cocaine.

In one corner was a stripper's pole. Grand opulence upstairs, Stripper motif downstairs. The American dream.

Gina walked across the room to one of the purple velvet couches and shook a not-quite completely naked man awake.

"Shane. Shane, wake up."

"Mmmgmmn," the not-quite completely naked man said.

"Shane."

He opened his eyes this time. "Gina." He tried to sit up, but something inside his head told him to stop. "Oh god." He laid his head back down on the purple velvet.

"Shane, these people are looking for some dude who might have been here last night."

Shane looked at us. This time he succeeded in sitting up. He looked down at the floor. He looked up at us. He reached for a glass on the mirror table with yellow-ish liquid in it. He put the glass under his nose and sniffed it.

"Whiskey," he said happily, and downed it in a quick gulp.

His whole body shook.

He looked at us again. "That's a little better," he said. "So, uh, who you looking for?"

"His name's IQ. It's really Izzy, but he goes by IQ," Stella said. "Six feet tall, short dark hair. He's our drummer."

Shane didn't respond at first. He seemed lost in thought. Then he casually asked, "Was he wearing a plain white t-shirt? Sleeveless, like it showed his awesome shoulder muscles?"

"Yes!" Stella said.

Shane looked up. "He was here."

Stella knelt down to look at Shane face to face. "What can you tell me?"

"He didn't seem like he was having much fun for a while. But eventually he loosened up. He hooked up with a couple girls. Oh, shit, sorry. You his girlfriend?"

"No," Stella said. "I'm not. How late was he here?"

"Shit," Shane said, "we were still at it this morning. What time is it?"

Shane looked across the room at a clock. "Six-thirty! Fuck. Hey where's my phone?"

"Look," said Stella, "can you tell me about these girls? Where would we find them?"

"Come with me," he said. "They're gonna be at my show." He wandered around the room looking under tables, in corners, scratching his head in bewilderment.

"Your show?" Stella asked. "Where? When?"

"Right now," he said. "I got to hit it."

"What kind of show?"

"I'm D-J-ing. It's a warehouse. Gonna get crazy. A couple guys rapping. Then a band's gonna play. Everyone's gonna be there."

"Where?"

"Downtown. You can follow me. There it is." He bent down and pulled his phone out from under a purple velvet couch. Tapping the screen, he said "fuck" two or three times, and then put it to his ear.

"Nate!...shit man, I just woke up...no fucking way, man. I'm on my way...the show must go on, baby...A'ight...A'ight, cool...Out." He hung up and looked at us. "You comin'?"

"How about I ride in your car?" I said, glancing at Stella. "That way I can make sure no one gets lost."

"Let's go," he said.

I regretted the suggestion almost as soon as it came out of my mouth.

I regretted it even more when I closed the passenger door to Shane's brand new BMW. He reached across me to the glove compartment, opened it, and pulled out a small baggie of white powder. He scooped his finger nail into it, put it under his nose and snorted. Apparently he always kept a backup supply of cocaine in the car.

He started the car up, shifted, hit the button that opens the gate, and in about three seconds we were ten miles away. Physically, at least. It took a few minutes for my brain to catch up with the car.

When I finally got my bearing I was surprised we weren't wrapped around a tree.

As we flew along the PCH Shane turned to me and said, "So, what are you, some old rock and roll dude?"

"How old do you think I am?" I asked.

"I don't know. Forty five? Fifty?"

"I'm sorry I asked. I'm a drummer."

"You probably hate hip hop."

"No, man, I'm a drummer. A drummer can't hate hip hop. It's like the ultimate evolution of the art of rhythm."

"Cool," he said. "Maybe you're alright."

"Don't you think you should eat something, man?" I asked. "You just woke up, and so far all you've had is whiskey and cocaine for breakfast."

"Oh, shit. you ARE an old fart," he said.

"I've seen a couple people in my life die, is all," I said.

"Live fast. Die young. Leave a good looking corpse."

"That's stupid. No one gives a fuck what your corpse looks like," I said. "All anyone's gonna know is that you fucked up and died."

"This is not a rock and roll attitude," he said.

"Well, man, like I said, I've seen a couple people die."

Shane laughed. "What's a midlife crisis like?" he asked.

"Hell if I know," I said. "I don't know anything about midlife or early life or late life. The only question I ask myself every morning is; am I alive or am I dead? If I'm alive, then I just get up and go do something."

"And if you're dead?" Shane was looking at me with a mischievous grin.

"Well," I said, "I guess I would take that as a sign to stop."

Shane laughed.

I received a text from Stella asking where I was.

"Just take the 10 downtown. Will tell you where it is when we get there," I sent back.

The Warehouse

The place was huge and echo-y, with maybe twenty people walking around. Things would get crazy in a couple hours, everyone said.

I sent Stella the directions, and accepted a beer from a twenty-something guy in a suit and loosened tie.

"I'm Nate," he said, holding out his hand.

"Zenny."

"You sure this is your scene? It's gonna get wild in here tonight."

"No, it's probably not my scene," I said. "But that's okay. If the music's good I can handle it."

A loud electronic pulse pounded through the cavernous room, as Shane and two other guys checked their equipment.

A drum set stood behind them.

"What do you do?" Nate asked me.

"Drummer," I said. "You?"

"I'm an equity management broker."

"Equity Manage-. Holy fuck!"

"I make people rich," he said.

"You ever make anyone poor along the way?" I asked.

Nate laughed. "Of course. Dog eat dog, you know."

I took a swig of my beer and looked out at the empty warehouse. "Isn't that cannibalism?"

"What?"

"Dogs eatin' dogs?"

He laughed again "You better believe it is. That's what makes the world go around."

"Well, it seems like, for a lot of those dogs, the world stops going around."

I stood up and walked toward the front of the room.

Shane was testing a variety of sounds and electronic rhythms.

Without asking I walked to the drum set and looked at it.

Shane's sound wall was intensifying. It had a hip hop rhythm to it that I kind of liked. I thought that this would be a good time to shake off a little bit of the rust.

I sat on the stool and picked up two drum sticks that were resting on the floor tom.

The snare was about a half inch higher than I like, but I decided not to adjust someone else's kit.

Shane's electronic pulse shook the room.

Boom, boom boom boom.

I joined in.

Simple at first. I just kept the main beat with the high hat, dropping the off-beat on the snare.

I looked up at Shane. He was bobbing his head in sync with the beat. He looked over at me, still bobbing his head. Then a smile played across his face.

I stayed on the beat, but changed from the high hat to the first cymbal. I didn't like the sound of that cymbal, and switched to the other.

Then I started having fun, and so did Shane. I played around with some fills, challenging myself to play chicken with the beat, but never lose it.

Shane flipped a switch and a sound like a psychedelic pipe organ filled the room.

A guy who'd been hanging around Shane started smiling and walked to a microphone, shaking his body and shoulders in rhythm. He grabbed the mic and started rapping.

I couldn't hear what he was rapping about. It didn't matter. The rhythm was all that mattered. I was enjoying it. The three of us made eye contact the way musicians are supposed to. It felt good to lose myself in a moment with two guys I'd never even met before. Sometimes it works, and when it does, it reminds you why you're a musician.

We went on like that, improvising, for about five minutes, playing off each other like teammates on a basketball court.

When we finally brought it to an end, everyone smiled and nodded.

Then I realized I should probably quit while I'm ahead. Shane and the guys still had a lot of setting up to do.

I stepped down off the stage and saw Stella, Andre, and GQ entering the far end of the warehouse.

A bouncer stopped them. Stella was gesticulating and pointing toward me. The bouncer was shaking his head. Stella looked heated.

I looked back at Shane. He saw me, looked out across the warehouse, saw what was going on, and shouted, "S'a'ight, Cooper. you can let those three in."

Across the room the bouncer nodded, and Stella, GQ and Andre began walking towards me.

"Not bad."

It was Nate again.

"Hey, man, thanks," I said.

"Let me give you my card," he said, pulling a small business card from his wallet. I took it and looked at it.

"I don't know if I'd be a very useful client to you," I said.

"You want to be rich, don't you?" he asked.

I thought about this for a moment. "It's not something I think about much," I finally said.

"Come on. Everyone wants to be rich. Admit it. What do you really want more than anything else in the world?"

"What do I want, more than anything else?" I repeated.

"Yeah."

"I want peace of mind, man."

"What?"

"I want peace of mind. I want to calm my brain down. I want to sleep, to start a dream, and finish it."

"That's weird," Nate said. "That's really weird. Everyone else in this world wants to be rich."

Stella, Andre, and GQ finally made it across the enormous empty room.

"Why are we here?" Stella asked.

"Well, Shane thinks the girls IQ hooked up with will be here tonight."

"This is a fucking wild goose chase."

"Any word from the cops?"

"No," Stella said. "Talked to Officer Nazi Asshole on the way here. Nothing."

We shook our heads, and shrugged.

"Friends of yours?" Nate asked.

"Yeah," I said. "Stella and the band. Everyone, this is Nate. He makes some people rich and a few people poor, and he approves of dog cannibalism."

Nate laughed. Stella and the guys looked confused. Nate held out his hand to Stella.

"Good to meet you," he said.

"Hi."

"Pleasure," he said to Andre.

"Cool," Andre said.

GQ shook his hand but didn't say anything.

Stella looked at her watch. "So...when do things get started around here?"

"Couple hours," Nate said.

Stella looked at me, and said, "So...what, are we just going to sit around and wait?"

Chapter Five

Dancing With Whoever

We just sat around and waited.
For two hours.
Then people began arriving.
Waves of scantily-clad girls, guys in tank tops thinking they're the shit.
There's something about 20-year-old girls screaming hello to each other that hurts my ears. I was relieved when Shane started the music and drowned out the screaming girls.
If you're ever among a large group of people, wondering what they think of you, just remember this one thing; They couldn't care less about you. They are worried about one thing and one thing only….what everyone else thinks of THEM.
Soon the empty warehouse was packed with more people than it could fit.
Shane and his crew were pounding out beats from so many speakers the whole warehouse was pulsing.
"How are we going to find two girls we've never met?" Stella asked.
I looked over at her. "I guess we ask each and every girl if they spent last night with IQ."
She half-smiled and shook her head.
"I'll be in the bar," I said.
"We'll come find you."
I made my way toward the back of the room. I had to squeeze my way through dozens of young bodies.
People were dancing with abandon, and the night had only just begun.
As I twisted and turned my way through, I was almost forced to dance with one girl. I swear I was just trying to get past her, but

there was no room. She gyrated and danced closer to me. She pushed her pelvis against my hip. Her eyes were only half open. Then she finally looked at my face and did a quick double-take, like the lines in my face caught her by surprise. She wasn't expecting a guy with lines in his face. But her eyes glazed over again and she was in her own world, inside her own head. She didn't care who she danced with, and wouldn't remember me.

I moved on past her and finally made my way to the bar.

"Whatever beer's the cheapest," I said to the bartender, and sat on a stool.

The bartender put a beer in front of me and I took a swig.

"Hey man."

I turned. It was Nate again.

"Hey."

"Pretty crazy, huh."

"Yeah," I said. "I was almost forced to have sex on my way through the crowd just now.'

"You haven't seen anything yet. Just wait."

"So, why are you here?" I asked. "Is this really your scene? I mean, you know, you got the whole suit and tie thing going."

"It's my show," he said.

"I thought it was Shane's show."

"I put up the money for this," he said, waving his hands around to indicate the warehouse.

"Really? You made this happen?"

"I did."

"You make money on this? All these screaming girls paying to strut their stuff?"

"Sure do. I wouldn't keep doing it if it didn't make a profit. I mean, what would be the point of that?"

"Hm? Of what?"

"What would be the point of doing something that doesn't make a profit?"

"I don't know," I said. "Maybe the point would be to do it, you know, just to do it. But what the fuck do I know?"

"The only reason to do anything is for me to make money," Nate said. "And I'm going to make a fucking shit load of it."

"Are you?"

"You watch, I'm planning to shape the fucking culture, man. I'm making plans to be a mogul, music, movies, you name it."

"You want to be a billionaire," I said dryly.

"A billionaire. A billionaire is chump change. The first billion is just the start of something really big."

I didn't really feel like having this conversation. Money people talking about money has always bored me. I turned out toward the crowd and watched some of the girls dance.

"Hey, let's get you back up on those drums," Nate said.

"You sure Shane's down with that?"

"Absolutely. You saw how much he loved it."

"I don't know, man."

"Fuck it, it's my show," he said. "Come on."

He started walking out of the bar, turned to face me. "Come on."

I downed my beer in a gulp and followed him into the crowd.

I would say it was an enjoyable experience to squeeze between body after body, but most them were unaware of my presence.

I did unfortunately get a few of those dreaded looks this time; the look that says, "What's rock-and-roll-burnout doing here?"

I ignored the looks and followed Nate through the crowd toward the stage.

As I squeezed between a group of people, trying to ignore the butt touches and crotch taps, a girl facing away from me, dancing wildly, suddenly seemed to trip, staggered sideways, and threw her arm around me, catching herself from falling.

"Wooo!" she wailed, hanging onto me.

She didn't lose a beat in her dancing, and began gyrating with her arms around my neck.

I didn't want to join her at first, but she was holding me so close, I could only think of the Groucho Marx line, "If I was any closer I'd be in back of you."

I gave in, and we came as close to having sex as two people can while still wearing clothes.

In the middle of this deeply meaningful and intimate moment I felt a tapping on my shoulder. It was Nate.

He gestured with his head. I looked down into my new girlfriend's face. We smiled at each other and she removed her arms from around me.

I stepped away from her, as she turned and wrapped an arm around the next available guy, some 20-something asshole who wouldn't know how to make her happy if he wanted to.

"Oh well," I thought, turning to follow Nate through the crowd, "another quick romance and break-up. The story of my life."

Nate and I finally made it to the stage, where Shane was bobbing his head, lost completely in his own musical moment. His eyes were closed. He held headphones tight to his ears, concentrating on his next transition.

The moment came and he flashed his eyes open, hitting some switches on his console on quick succession, changing the rhythm and sending a wave of psychedelia out over the crowd.

Nate was tugging at my arm. He was gesturing toward the drums. I wanted to wait until we actually got a nod from Shane, but Shane kept his closed, lost in his trance. I gave in and climbed up to the drums.

I let Shane's funky psychedelic groove sink into me for a moment, and then joined in.

It felt good.

Shane turned and finally gave me the nod that told me it was alright, and then we hit it pretty hard.

If those people were dancing with abandon before, we took them to a whole new level.

Allie

I guess this was the guy who owned the drum kit. He was suddenly standing to my right. When I looked up, he nodded at me, indicating that he wanted to sit where I was sitting.

I understood, handed him his sticks, got up off the stool and jumped down off the stage.

He sat down and hit the beat a little more ferociously than I had.

The whole warehouse seemed to be bobbing up and down on its foundation.

I stepped back into the crowd thinking that it was a good time to try to catch up with Andre and Stella.

This time I tried squeezing my way around the edge of the crowd. I wanted to avoid any more short-term relationships. But once again an arm was suddenly around my neck.

"You're a good drummer."

She looked a few years older than the rest of them, 30-something, beautiful, brunette, a brain in her head. I liked her instantly.

"Oh, thanks, sorry," I said awkwardly.

"You in a band?"

"Well...yes and no."

"What do you mean?" she asked.

I was distracted by the faint glimpse of Stella's hair at the back of the room.

"Sorry," I said, "I was looking for someone."

"Male or female?"

"Both," I said. "One female, two males, the band I'm both in and not in."

She laughed. "Can I come with you?"

I thought for a quick second and said yes.

I started squeezing through the crowd again, and felt her grab ahold of my hand.

We finally reached the back of the warehouse, but I couldn't find Stella. I peered back across the top of the crowd.

"What do they look like?"

Then I saw her; Stella was dancing with her own arms wrapped around the neck of another girl.

"I can help look," I heard my new companion say.

I looked at Stella as she and her new dance partner kissed, kissed again, then started making out while continuing to grind together. So much for finding IQ, I thought. Derailed by. .by THIS.

"You know what," I said, "Fuck it, let's have a drink."

Still holding hands, we made our way to the bar and found two empty stools.

"What do you drink?"

"Rum and Coke," she said.

I turned to the bartender. "Rum and Coke, and a Jack on the rocks."

"Thanks."

"What's your name?" I asked.

"Allie."

"Hi, Alley. I'm Zenny."

"Hi."

We smiled at each other.

Then a voice came from the other side of Allie. "Gupper Fish," the voice said.

I leaned to look past Allie, and saw a 40-something woman with that face you only see in L.A.

Now, I have to be careful how I say this. I admit I am a middle aged guy. I want to avoid getting into the older-guy-younger-girl argument. There are middle aged women who are attractive. But what will never ever be attractive, is "The _.A. Face."

"The L.A. Face" is a middle aged face that has been botoxed up, surgically altered, lips injected, and generally presents a statement of fake bullshit....wait...do I mean REAL bullshit? I don't know. I definitely mean bullshit.

The one thing that is necessary to make a slightly older female face attractive is honesty. Let me see your real face. Let me see your real hair color. Don't hide behind a wall of bullshit.

The woman sitting at the bar on the other side of Allie, had a face like Frankenstein's monster. She had, I had to admit, said the name of my former band, though, and this roused some curiosity in me.

I leaned forward.

"Zenny Zeller," she said. "You were the drummer for Gupper Fish."

"I'm surprised you remember the band," I said. "I'm really surprised you remember I was the drummer."

"Well," she said, taking a sip from a tall glass, "I remember fucking you."

I quickly moved my hand to my mouth to prevent a swallow of beer from spraying all over the bar.

Glancing at Allie, I saw her smiling, enjoying my awkwardness.

"It's alright," the woman continued. "I guess I was just a groupie to you."

"Look," I said, unsure what to say at all, "No, I'm sorry. I'm, hey, it's um, it's good to, to finally -"

"Oh, fuck you," she said. "You're an asshole, like all of them." She stood and began to leave, stopped, reached back for her drink and drained it. She looked at Allie and said, "Dump him now. You can do so much better." Then she looked at me. "Your second album sucked. I'm glad you guys broke up."

"Be careful with your face," I yelled as she walked out of the bar. "If anything touches it, it could break."

Allie was laughing as I sat down next to her. I sighed and took a drink.

"Do you remember her?" Allie asked.

"Good question." I thought back through my memory banks. It's not as if I slept with hundreds of groupies. The Gupper Fish heyday lasted a total of about nine months, but those nine months are a total blur.

"No," I said.

Allie laughed. "What's your new band?"

"Hm? No, it's not my band. I just, uh, how can I explain it? I'm sort of the step-uncle of a dysfunctional family. They live in my house."

I was secretly hoping that would be enough to satisfy her, but of course it wasn't.

"What are you doing here? Looking after the kids?"

"The drummer's missing."

"Aren't you the drummer?"

"No," I said. "I mean, yes, sometimes, but I'm not the official drummer."

"So you're here to find him?"

"Well…" I took another drink. "I think the trail's run cold."

She looked at me and turned her head a little bit sideways. "What else do you do with your time?"

"Oh, you know…I'm always doing something. I….I s eep, I have these dreams."

"What about when you're awake?"

"I sit on the floor."

I realized that this brief reference to Zenny-med would probably leave her confused.

"You sit on the floor?"

"Yeah, you should try it. It's great."

"Anything else?"

"I bought a bike recently. Planning to start biking around town instead of driving. You know, exercise and all that."

She took a drink.

"Sorry," I said.

"For what?"

"For not being more interesting."

"Oh, you're interesting," she said.

"It's alright," I said. "You can go find some hotter younger guy. I'll live."

"I'm not attracted to little 20-year-old boys," she said. "Tell me more about this dysfunctional family of yours."

"It's not actually a family."

"I get that. Tell me about them."

"Well, first there's Stella. We're all kind of in love with Stella."

Allie opened her eyes a little wider. I continued.

"Right now Stella is out on that dance floor, making out with a girl."

"And you're upset about that?" Allie said.

"Hell no. I'm not upset about that. Stella can make out with girls or guys, or whatever else there is. In fact it sort of makes sense, if you know Stella. Explains a thing or two. I'm not upset."

"So, what's the problem?"

"Hm? Problem?"

"What's the dysfunction?"

"Oh that," I said. "I don't even know where to start. Just because she's out there making out with some girl, doesn't mean any of us are less in love with her. I"m in love with her. IQ's in love with her. Andre's in love with her. I don't know about GQ. He doesn't talk much. And it's a band, you know. Being in a band is like being married to three or four other people, but without the intimate moments, just the fights."

"Hm." Allie was looking into her beer, trying to process everything.

"How about you?" I asked. "What do you do?"

She stared off at nothing for a moment, took a drink and said, "I work in advertising, and I want to either quit or shoot myself."

"Well, at least you've identified what your options are."

She laughed.

"What brought you here, tonight?" I asked.

"My friend Rachel. She's out there dancing with some idiot."

"You have a boyfriend?"

"Why do you ask?"

I looked sideways at her. "I'm collecting data. It's a government study. Calculate the percentage of girls who do and don't have boyfriends."

She laughed again. I liked her laugh. "Good luck with that," she said. "And yes, I have a boyfriend. Or had. Or am breaking up with him."

"Okay," I said.

"Okay? What do you mean by 'okay'?"

"It makes a little more sense now."

"What makes sense?"

"I've been too many girls' rebound. I can smell the signs."

"You can smell the signs? What do the signs smell like?"

"A combination of paprika and dirty socks."

She smiled. "So...are you saying you do or don't want to be my rebound?"

"Do you want me to be?"

"For tonight."

"Alright," I said. "I'm your rebound. You can introduce me that way - 'Hi, this is Zenny. He's my rebound for tonight.'"

She smiled a little broader this time. It was an open, happy smile with honesty in it."

I couldn't help myself. I leaned forward and kissed her, just a quick little peck. I felt her soft lips tap mine for a split second. I liked it.

I leaned back. She gently put her hand on my upper arm.

"So, Zenny Zeller, that's your name, right."

"Right."

"Wanna go dance?"

"I can try," I said. "I'm not much of a dancer. I'm usually on drums when everyone else is dancing."

"You'll be fine," she said.

She took my hand and pulled me out toward the dance floor.

The show was in full rave mode. Not my natural scene, as Nate had pointed out earlier, but I wasn't going to complain.

And almost as soon as I started dancing with Allie, I stopped suddenly.

Allie stopped and looked at me, puzzled. Then she turned to look where I was looking.

"Yours?" she asked.

"Yes."

Across the room, in stark contrast to the happy delirium going on around them, Stella and Andre were arguing.

The music was pounding so loudly, I wondered how they could even hear each other. Andre's mouth opened and closed energetically. Stella's squawked open and closed with angry passion. Hands gestured in the air. Shoulders and heads shrugged and shook.

Then Andre threw a dismissive hand in the air and turned away from Stella, walking angrily toward the door.

Stella followed him. The beautiful girl Stella had been kissing also followed.

"Doesn't look good," Allie said.

"Nope."

I dropped my head and began walking. Allie followed me. Fighting through the crowd, I found myself thinking that I didn't want to be mediator between Stella and Andre.

I stopped. Allie stopped. I thought for a moment.

"Fuck it," I said "Let 'em fight."

I turned back toward the dance floor. I put my hand on her shoulder and she followed me again.

Then I stopped again. I knew I had to go work on Stella and Andre.

"Aw fuck!" I said and began walking back toward the door of the warehouse.

Allie was laughing at my indecision.

When I finally made it to the door, I pushed it open and walked out into the peaceful night air. It would have been peaceful, anyway, if Andre and Stella weren't yelling the peacefulness into submission.

"That is such fucking bulshit!" Andre was yelling as I came out. "What do you do every time I have an idea?"

"I fucking listen," Stella yelled. "No matter how stupid or bizarre, or completely mind-fuckingly ridiculous it is, I listen."

"And then you do your 'whatever' thing."

"What 'whatever' thing?"

"Your 'whatever' thing," Andre repeated. "You do it all the time. You nod and look at me, and I know my idea is dead on arrival, and then you do your 'whatever' thing."

"I don't do my 'whatever' thing. I don't fucking have a 'whatever' thing I don't even know what a fucking 'whatever' thing fucking is."

"I think maybe it's finally time," Andre said.

"Time for what?" Stella yelled.

"Time to fucking break this sorry joke of a band up."

"Oh fuck you. What are you gonna do on your own? You'll come crawling back, begging."

I sighed and looked behind me. Allie was standing just outside the door, fascinated by this display of childishness.

Then I began slowly walking toward Andre.

"I'm sorry," Andre was saying, "if I'm not a member of the cult of Stella anymore."

I walked right up to him and looked him in the eye. I grabbed his shoulder and pulled him away with me.

"Maybe you should think about taking a step back," said. "Maybe sleep on this. Take a deep breath. It's been a long day."

"I'm done with it, Zenny," he said. "I've taken all I can fucking take."

"Just sleep on it, Andre. That's all I ask."

"She's fucking crazy."

"Of course she is. And so am I, and so are you."

"Don't include me in that group," he said.

"Oh, you're crazy," I said. "You're fucking looney tunes. How else do you think you got to be so brilliant?"

"Zenny, what the fuck are you talking about?"

"You're nuts, Andre. Always have been. And you're brilliant. I mean, normal people don't have the wild symphonies of music going on inside them that you have. It makes you crazy, because you can't turn the music off. When you were a kid you believed you were another Mozart, another Gershwin, another Jimi Hendrix. Hell, you thought you were better than them. You became a pretentious fuck, but I love you, and so does Stella, even if she won't admit it right now. I want you crazy, because that's the real you, and I want to hear the brilliant music that you haven't played yet, that you'll play sometime in the future."

"But we're not talking about me, are we."

"No...no, we're not. We're talking about Stella. And everything I just said about you, I could say the same about Stella. You know why you two fight so much? It's not because you're so wildly different from each other. It's because you're too similar. I mean, fuck, the two of you are so alike sometimes, it's eerie."

Andre broke into a quiet, derisive chuckle. "Nice try, Zenny," he said. "I'm fucking out."

He turned and walked down the street. He kept walking until he disappeared into the darkness.

When I turned around Stella was wiping tears off her face. The girl she was with tried to console her. Allie was standing alone a short distance away.

I walked toward Stella. As I got close she looked up at me, trying to gather her emotions together. I put my arms around her, and she leaned her head onto my chest.

"Sorry," she said.

"It's alright," I said. "What started it?"

"He wanted to take the keys to the van. He wanted to leave us here."

She sniffled and pulled out of the hug, rubbing the moisture off her face.

"I guess we don't have to worry about the fucking show tomorrow," she said. "God, why is everything so fucked up?"

"Tomorrow's another day," I said. "Don't assume you know what will happen tomorrow."

Stella looked at me like I was crazy. Then my eye caught the girl she was with.

"Hi, I'm Tam."

"Good to meet you, Tam. I'm Zenny."

I reached my hand toward Allie. Allie walked closer and took my hand.

"This is Allie," I said.

"Hi,"

"Good to meet you."

"Likewise."

"Well, what now?" Stella asked.

"Any idea where GQ is?"

"No idea," said Stella. "He could be anywhere."

Walking Away

I sat in the back of the cab with Allie, thinking about what a long, crazy day it had been.

I'd been on the move all day, wishing I could get just one moment to sit still. I felt a pain settling into the right side of my neck.

"What are you thinking about?" Allie asked.

"I was just sitting here thinking that I never had a moment all day to just sit and think."

"Do you think the band is really over?"

"No," I said, "but I don't think we're going to be able to find IQ."

"Why not?"

"I don't think he wants to be found."

"Why do you think that?"

"I don't think he's missing. I think he decided to drop out. He'll come back when he decides to come back, and not a moment sooner."

"Has he done anything like this before?"

"Yes," I said. "I was talking to his brother once. GQ doesn't talk much, but one day we were hanging out, and he told me some things."

"Like what?"

"As a kid IQ was one of those computer savants. You know, the next Bill Gates or Steve Jobs."

"Is that why everyone calls him IQ?"

"Well, those are his initials, but it fits. So, he's ten, eleven years old, on track to get into college at fifteen. People are writing news articles about him. Then, one day when he's thirteen, he drops out of school."

"What?"

"He dropped out of school. He quit. Eventually they got him back into school, but he was never the same. No interest in technology."

"Just like that?"

"Just like that," I said.

"Is that when he got into music?"

"GQ said he started taking drum lessons then, but his real obsession was to be an actor."

"Talk about losing your way."

"No, GQ said, and I believe him, that he was a brilliant actor. Did plays, a couple TV pilots where he played the teenager with an attitude."

"Any shows I would know?"

"No, nothing he did ever got picked up. But GQ says he was brilliant, and I don't doubt it."

"So," Allie scrunched up her face, trying to understand. "What happened to the acting, then?"

"He walked away from it."

"Weird."

"He never talks about it. By the time I met him, he was a badass drummer, one of the best I've ever seen."

"So, what, you think now he's just walking away from drumming?"

"I think this time he's walking from everything; drumming, this band, Stella, his brother. He probably didn't lose his wallet. He probably threw it in the bushes on purpose. Probably tossed his cell phone out the window of that damn limousine."

"Why would someone do that?"

"That's the first step to freedom."

"Hm?"

"I mean, according to his mind. No wallet, no identification, no way for anyone to contact you. That's stepping out of the cage into the wild jungle. It's either freedom or death, you know, you either survive by your wits or you get eaten."

"But, why?" Allie was genuinely trying to understand someone she had never met. "What does it get you? What's he searching for?"

"I think he's searching for some kind of life this normal world doesn't offer."

I looked at Allie. She smiled at me.

"And now here I am," I said, "riding in a cab with you. And I don't even really know who you are."

"Are you having second thoughts about me?"

"Hell no, I'm not having second thoughts about you "

She gave me a happy smile. Then she leaned over and gave me a kiss.

"How come everyone you know is both brilliant and completely crazy?"

"I'm not very good at normal," I said. "Normal people -"

"What?" she asked.

"Nothing," I said. "I like normal people, too. I just get along better with the crazy ones."

Issues Of Her Own

Women are mind-boggling.

Some like to be treated one way. Some like to be treated the opposite way.

Some like things slow. Some like things fast.

Some want you to look at them, and desire them. Others will never speak to you again if you look at them with desire.

So, I've quit trying to guess.

I just assume that when a woman likes me, it's based on some fundamental misunderstanding, and that the countdown is on until she becomes disappointed in me.

It doesn't really matter what I do or don't do.

Allie's apartment was refreshingly normal. She lived in a one-bedroom. There was just enough clutter - some clothes tossed randomly, knick knacks knocked over - to make me like her more.

Allie closed the door and turned to me. We smiled dumbly at each other for a moment.

"You live here alone?" I asked.

"Yeah."

"What about the guy you're leaving?"

"He wants to move in, wants us to live together."

She was close to me. I felt her breath on my cheek as she spoke.

I let my lips tap hers.

It was nice.

She pressed her body against mine. I felt her breasts pushing gently against me.

Our kiss started slow, then became more intense.

She began unbuttoning her blouse. She turned and walked away from me, tossing her blouse on the couch. I stared at the baby blue bra strap across her back.

She shimmied out of her pants, to reveal matching baby blue panties.

She turned and looked at me, smiling. I smiled back and walked toward her.

I knew she had planned this before she ever went out for the evening.

She was going to get a guy tonight. Someone. For her own reasons.

Sheer dumb luck had fallen on me. It could have been any other dumb guy at Shane's show.

I didn't mind.

She had issues of her own to work out, and I was happy to help.

As I approached her, I slid my hands across the soft skin of her waist, and I marveled at how alive her skin felt.

We locked lips.

And the rest is my fucking secret.

Chapter Six

Goal

I was running with a soccer ball at my feet. I was running as fast as I could.

I could see the goal up ahead, and ran toward it, dribbling the ball. It was getting harder and harder to breathe. I was huffing and puffing.

I looked ahead toward the goal, and realized it was getting further away.

Impossible! How can it be? I was running toward it, step after step, dribbling the ball, but with every step the goal moved further away from me.

But I just kept running.

And running and running.

I looked up again, and the goal was so far away, it had nearly disappeared into the distance.

I was stumbling now. I had been running for so long, I was out of breath and my legs felt like rubber.

But I just kept running, stumbling forward, dribbling the ball in front of me.

I looked up toward the goal again, and it was not there anymore.

Gone.

Then I heard him coming up behind me; a big, stocky, athletic, beast of a man, pounding his feet on the ground, catching up to me.

He was getting closer and closer, and he wanted the ball.

Focus! I still have some moves left in me. He'll never get this ball.

Then, from right behind me he let out a beastly growl and –

"Zenny!"

Crap crap crap!

It was Allie.

Another dream interrupted.

This is becoming a very serious problem.

"Zenny!"

"Do you have any idea how close I am to losing my mind right now?"

She looked at me with mild concern, and said, "I have to meet someone. I called you a cab."

I sat up and rubbed my eyes. "Will I see you again?" I asked.

She looked down.

The silence said everything there was to say.

"You've been a breath of fresh air," she said.

I thought for a moment, trying to understand what the hell this meant.

She stood up.

"The cab's outside," she said.

She doesn't waste any time.

Complete Mess

On the cab ride home, I watched the world pass by the car window, not feeling much of anything.

IQ was still missing and, I suspected, wanted to stay missing.

I, for some reason, love a girl way too young for me, who everybody else also loves, and who is probably right now waking up naked next to a naked girl.

A show that was supposed to happen tonight seemed unlikely to happen.

I was still running out of money.

And my head was a complete mess.

Because We're Human

I unlocked the door to the house and walked in to a very silent kind of silence. The house was empty, completely empty.

I rummaged around in the fridge for a minute, grabbed a couple of cheese sticks, and sat down on the beat up living room couch.

I decided I should at least try to contact the band, so I sent out the same text to Stella, Andre, and GQ:

"Where are you?"

I sat and stared at nothing for a few minutes. Then the front door opened and Stella stood in the door frame. She closed the door slowly, and moved toward me without saying anything. Her head was down. She looked tired and depressed.

She sat down next to me on the couch, and tucked her feet up under her. She reached her hand across me and put it on my shoulder. Then she laid her head against my chest and curled up.

I put an arm around her.

My phone vibrated.

GQ responded, "On my way."

"Anything from Andre?" Stella asked.

"Nothing yet."

"Why is everything so fucked up?"

"I don't know," I said. "Maybe it's because we're human."

She lifted her head off my chest, rubbed her eyes, and sniffled.

"Is there any way this show can be salvaged tonight?"

"Maybe," I said.

She slowly stood up. "Come get me if anything happens."

She walked off down the hall.

Great Wall

I don't know if it was The Great Wall of China, or just some random really high, really impressive wall. It was huge, though, and I was on top of it.

On both sides the wall stretched down and down forever.

My vertigo kicked in. I hate heights. I get a queasy, unbalanced feeling, and get light headed.

On one side of the wall was a narrow staircase that went all the way down, so I stepped onto the top and went down twenty-five or thirty steps. Then I realized how far down it was and that there was no handrail, and that I was certain to fall off before I got to the bottom.

I began feeling sick. I panicked. I turned to go back up the way I came.

No, that's no good either. I'll be stuck on this damn wall forever!

I have to get off this wall, and I have to get off these steps.

And I knew I had to do it before someone woke me up. I knew it was a dream, and I was panicked anyway.

I looked up toward the top of the wall. Then I looked down at the vast distance I would fall if I fell off.

I - I -

"Zenny!"

Fucking hell!

I opened my eyes, still shaking from fear.

It was GQ.

"You alright, man?" he asked.

"The wall - the steps."

"What? Zenny, wake up. You're mumbling nonsense."

"Is it too much to ask that a guy get to sleep until he's done sleeping?"

"Come on," GQ said. "Pull yourself together."

I sighed. "What time is it?"

"Four O'clock."

"What!?"

"It's four O'clock."

"How the fuck did it get so late?"

"I don't know, Zenny," GQ said. "I guess time never stopped to wait for you."

"I dropped my head into my hands. "What time is the sound check supposed to be?"

"I have no idea," he said.

"How are we going to do a sound check," - it was Stella slowly walking down the hall toward us, "when we're missing so much of the band."

Neither GQ or I had an answer, so we didn't say anything.

Stella grabbed a glass from the shelf, and poured water into it from the kitchen faucet.

She walked into the living room, sat in a chair, took a sip of her water, and quietly said, "Fuck."

She tapped her phone and put it to her ear.

"Who you calling?" I asked.

"Andre."

She listened for a moment, then said "fuck," again and tossed her phone across the room. It landed harmlessly on the couch next to me.

"He's right, you know," Stella said. "We can't do this without him. So much for impressing Glazer at Polymorph."

"We don't need assholes like Glazer," GQ said. "Not in this day and age. We can do everything ourselves."

Stella looked up at GQ. "Tell me something," she said. "How come you've been so calm?"

"What do you mean?"

"Your brother's gone missing. We've all been freaking out. you've been along for the ride, but you never seemed worried."

"It's just the way I am."

Stella looked at him quizzically and looked away. "And we do need assholes like Glazer at Polymorph," she said. "We've been doing everything ourselves for the last three years. I've been busting my butt, and I don't know about you, but I want more people to know we exist than 300 internet followers. Maybe you're happy with that. If so, you better go get a restaurant job, 'cause you're gonna have to wait tables in between practices.'

"She's right," I said.

"About what? The restaurant job, or the fact that she's been busting her butt?"

"Both."

"Have you ever met Glazer?" GQ asked.

"No, never met him. We used to have a guy named Rick Houseman. Talked out of his ass a lot, but he knew how to promote a fucking band. Glazer will probably feed us a line of 80 percent bulshit, but the 20 percent that's real is what you actually need...especially in this day and age. The average band is making less and less money every year. Too much is going out for free."

"Well, I think we can do it ourselves," GQ said calmly.

Stella looked at GQ and sighed.

"Give me my phone," she said. "I guess I have to call the club and cancel."

I reached to my right and picked her phone up off the couch cushion. As soon as I picked it up it went nuts. I looked at the screen and turned to Stella.

"Andre's calling," I said.

She turned her head sideways at me. I decided to answer it myself.

"Hello."

"H - hi, who's this? Zenny?"

"No," I said, "this is Stella. Who does it sound like?"

"Zenny, hey. Did I fuck up? Are we on for tonight?'

"Well," I said, looking across at Stella, "I think if you're there we'll all be there."

A silent pause.

"Alright, look, here's the deal. I'm in fucking Anaheim."

"Anaheim! How the hell did you end up in Anaheim?"

The Vortex

Sometimes in life you have to hurry up...and then you have to wait.

After talking to Andre, we decided we should load all our gear into the van and hit the freeway to Anaheim.

The plan was to get Andre, then go directly to the club. We had to have everything loaded into the van before heading to fucking Anaheim.

So we hurried.

And then we got on the freeway.

And we waited.

I do not believe that all the cars on the L.A. freeways are real.

I believe there is a time-space vortex in southern California, and at given times of the day, cars from other parts of the world transpose through the vortex and emerge in L.A.

Cars that are actually in Europe, Asia, South America, enter the vortex and, although they are still technically somewhere else in the world, they slow down L.A. traffic.

We were loaded up. We were on the freeway. We were surrounded by cars. We were not moving an inch.

"How did he end up in Anaheim, again?" Stella asked.

"Some girl," I said.

Stella sighed a weary sigh, and looked out at the traffic.

These crazy People

It was seven O'clock when we finally pulled up in front of a big bland expensive suburban Anaheim house.

I sent Andre a text; "We're here, I think."

When he didn't respond right away, I looked over at Stella. I could tell she didn't want to deal with this, so I got out the passenger door, and walked up to the house. The doorbell was one of those grand musical announcements that goes on and on, chiming some silly tune for a full minute.

Andre opened the door and came out, closing it quickly behind him.

"Thank god," he said. "I couldn't take anymore of those crazy people."

Then he saw the van and turned to face away from it.

"How bad is it?" he asked.

"Oh, I don't know," I said. "I think you both feel shitty about things you said to each other."

He breathed a heavy sigh and turned around, walking to the van.

Stella kept her gaze purposefully out the front window, avoiding any eye contact with Andre.

I got into the passenger seat. Andre opened the back door and sat between piles of gear.

Without saying anything, Stella started the engine and pulled away from the curb.

Ballet traffic Control

This was my first time in Anaheim in years. I had no idea where the hell we were. All I knew was that we were back on another freeway, and stuck in another vortex of stalled traffic.

The van was weirdly quiet. GQ and Andre both had their tiny speakers in their ears, each in their own secluded world of music.

Stella stared out the window at the traffic that wasn't moving, going over and over something in her own mind.

I decided I could take a moment to put my head together.

I took a deep breath, closed my eyes, and relaxed.

I began thinking about drumming. This was not an ideal situation for any of us. I still worried that I was rusty. I still worried that I didn't know the band's songs very well.

I worried that something bad would go down between Stella and Andre on stage.

I took another deep breath and chose to visualize everything going really fucking awesome.

"What the fuck!" Stella shouted.

I opened my eyes quickly.

She was pointing out the window to the freeway ahead of us.

No cars were moving. People were honking.

And then, several car lengths in front of us, I saw him; a man in pajamas and a court jester's hat, dancing across the lanes of the freeway, happy as could be.

He was dancing wildly. A couple cars tried to ease past him on the outside lanes, but he ran, or danced, quickly in front of them.

It was the most bizarre display of ballet traffic control I had ever seen. I wanted to think I was dreaming it, but it was really happening.

"That guy is fucking nuts," Stella said.

"How do you know? Maybe he's the only sane one. Maybe it's all the rest of us who are crazy."

She looked at me and laughed. "That guy is fucking nuts," she said.

I stared out at him. He was barely avoiding being hit by cars that were trying to get past him.

This was not going to end well, I realized, unless someone did something.

I wasn't really sure what my plan was, as I opened the door of the van, and stepped out onto the pavement of the freeway.

I walked calmly between cars, ignored all the honking, and walked up to the dancing man in pajamas.

He twirled for me, did a pirouette, spun several times across the lanes, and presented his hand to me.

I gave into the moment, and took his hand. Silently, we danced what must have looked like an idiots dance. I tried my best to lead him to the freeway shoulder. We twirled together to the right hand lane.

The cars in the left hand lanes began moving. This troubled my dance partner, but I held onto his hand and pulled him to the shoulder.

Traffic was moving again across all the lanes of the freeway. The man looked at me confused.

Then Stella eased the van to the shoulder and I led the confused man to the van. I opened the door and helped him in next to Andre. I sat in the passenger seat.

"Where we taking him?" Stella asked.

"I don't know. Just take the next exit."

She drove about a half-mile and took the exit. When we came to a stoplight at the end of the off ramp, I jumped out opened the back door and stood, waiting for him to get the message.

He never spoke.

He stepped slowly out onto the pavement.

I patted him on the shoulder.

Then suddenly and without warning he turned and began to run back toward the traffic, back up the off ramp toward the busy freeway.

I watched him go.

I closed the back door of the van, climbed back into the passenger seat, and looked over at Stella.

"Well," I said. "I tried."

"He's gonna get himself killed," she said.

I looked back at GQ and Andre. Each of them had remained closed off in their own worlds. Andre was asleep. GQ stared out the side window, listening to his music, oblivious to everything else in the world.

"Can you drive?" Stella asked. "I have to make a couple calls"

I stepped back out of the van, and Stella and I swapped places.

As I pulled the van back into traffic, Stella called the club to let them know where we were, and that we were on our way. Then she called Glazer's office to confirm his plan to be at the show.

Then she made a third call.

She sat with her phone to her ear, staring blankly ahead, listening.

She listened for about a minute, then took the phone away and swiped her finger across the screen.

I looked over at her. She had a slightly puzzled look.

"Who'd you call?"

"IQ."

I nodded and kept my eye on the road.

"His phone rang. It didn't go straight to voicemail."

I drove for a moment without responding.

"Maybe someone else found it," I said. "Maybe someone else is using IQ's phone."

"What do you think happened to him?" she asked. "Or, what's he up to? Or what….just what?"

I looked up at the rear view mirror at GQ. I felt like GQ knew something.

"Remember last time?" I asked.

"Of course I do."

"How did his brother react?"

"He didn't. He doesn't really react to anything, except a chord change."

"What goes on that kid's head?" I said.

Stella looked at GQ and quickly looked away. GQ noticed. He took the speaker out of his left ear and looked from Stella to me.

"What?" he asked.

"Nothing," Stella said.

He stared at us for a moment longer, then put his music back in and turned back to the window.

Then Andre woke up.

He blinked a couple times, sat up in the cramped space he'd been sleeping in, and glanced toward Stella. Their eyes caught each other for the briefest of moments. They each looked away immediately.

"Alright, everybody," I said. "Let's take a look at where we are."

I had Stella's attention. I had Andre's attention. I decided to continue on without GQ's.

"We're on a freeway, crawling so slow, we'll be lucky to get to the gig on time. We have me playing substitute drums, even though I don't really know your songs, because your regular drummer either; A) quit the band, quit his life, and disappeared, or B) took an unannounced vacation, or C) was kidnapped or killed or locked away somewhere. We have our mutual girlfriend Stella here…"

I looked at her, smiling.

"It's time for you to somehow come to grips," I continued, "with the fact that all the guys in your life, not some of us, not most of us, ALL of us are secretly completely in love with you. IQ certainly is, and you know as well as I do that that probably has something to do with why he's gone missing. Andre is certainly in love with you." I looked back at Andre through the rear view mirror. "Don't bother denying it, Andre. If it's true, it's true. I know I'm certainly in love with you. And I'm not even discussing the GIRLS who are in love with you too. Add to all of that, the fact that you and Andre, here, aren't talking to each other. Add the fact that you're trying to be an artist, an honest one, with principle, and with respect for your audience. Add the fact that you're trying to become successful in the totally impossibly fucked up music industry. You have the most important music mogul you could ever hope to come see you, coming to see you tonight, if we make it, where god-knows-what's going to happen. We have a bass player back there who doesn't talk."

I let a moment of quiet settle into the van.

"We all live in my house, that I won't be able to pay for in a couple more months. I haven't been able to think, to breath, to finish a fucking dream in days.

I looked over at Stella, then back at Andre.

Then I began to laugh.

They both looked at me with some concern.

"We have the fates right where we want them," I said between laughs. "Everything's lined up perfectly. Sometimes there's a fine line between jumping off a cliff, and breaking through to the amazing unknown. We're right there, on the edge of the cliff. It's either gonna be brilliant, or it's going to be our fucking doom. But you know what? It is what it is, man. It is what it fucking is."

GQ finally noticed something was going on. He removed the speakers from his ears. I had managed to get Stella and Andre, if not laughing, at least smiling.

"Step aside, everybody." I yelled. "There's a new band on its way, fronted by a beautiful woman, and backed up by a genius on guitar and keyboards, a washed up has-been drummer, and a non-verbal bass player."

I honked the horn wildly at the cars around us, howled like a coyote, and finally relaxed, shrugged my shoulders, and quietly pulled the van into a different lane.

GQ looked over at Andre. "What the fuck's wrong with Zenny?" he asked.

Chapter Seven

STAGE

We were supposed to start our set at 10:30.

By the time we won our battle with the traffic vortex, and pulled the van up behind the club, it was ten minutes after Ten.

The first band - they called themselves Event Horizon - had just finished.

There wasn't much time to think about anything. We just went to work loading the gear out of the van, and into the space next to the stage.

As Event Horizon got their gear off stage, we set ours up as fast as we could.

The business of setting up seemed to calm things down between Stella and Andre. It was something to do.

In many ways it felt like just another gig. Deep down, though, I believed what I had ranted about earlier in the van. This would be one of those nights you remember for the rest of your life. I just didn't know yet if it would be for good reasons or bad reasons.

Finally we were set up.

The crowd was energetic and happy. A few people in the front were real fans. Stella had a few die-hard fans, and they let her know how excited they were.

We didn't have a proper sound check, so Andre tried playing a random riff, to see how his monitor sounded. He was playing more than just a riff, I realized, and joined him, trying to gauge how much I could hear myself against the rest of the band.

Before we knew it, we were improvising a pretty goddamn funky song.

Stella and GQ joined us, and before long we were all smiling at each other.

We went on for three or four minutes, and found a way to wind it down together.

The crowd liked it.

An unexpected wave of cheering passed over us, and it felt good.

"Thanks," Stella said into the mic. "That's a new song. We just wrote it. It's called, 'Gettin' The Hell Outta Orange County.' "

A few more shouts and whistles from the crowd.

Then, just to cover some necessary business, Stella leaned into the mic again, and spoke to the sound guy at the back. "Turn up the bass," she said, "and my mic."

Then she turned around and looked at me. I glanced down at the sheet of paper I'd placed strategically to the left of my drum kit. It was the set list Stella wrote out earlier in the van.

The first song was called "Pulp Friction," and it started fast.

I nodded back to her, taped my sticks together, one - two - three - four and we were off.

We shredded that song sideways and upside down.

Andre was locked in.

GQ was solid.

I just tried to let it all flow through me.

Just let it flow, I told myself. Whatever happens, just let it flow. Be in the moment. Live this moment.

Watching Stella from behind is like getting a backstage pass to the sexuality charisma fair. I just marvel at her. And I'm kind of jaded. I've hung out with a lot of artists who were pretty impressed with themselves. Singers, lyricists, cultural icons who knew they were God's gift, and I grew tired of them all.

Stella, though, is the real thing. She's just this person. She doesn't play a character. She doesn't 'project' sexiness. She just puts her heart and soul out there for the audience to see, and they love her for it. They love her for it because they feel like they know her from her music.

What else do I feel when I watch Stella from behind? Well, all I admit to is what I've already said. I deny everything else you're thinking.

Andre is one of the rare ones. He has a way of playing guitar and keyboards at the same time.

He taps the guitar strings to the frets with the fingers of his left hand. He can make a guitar sing or cry this way.

At the same time, with his right hand, he can do almost any goddamn thing he wants on the keyboard.

The second song started like that; crying from the guitar balanced by a symphonic wall of sound from the keyboard.

Shit! When do I come in?

Fuck! I missed it.

Stella turned half-way toward me. She held her guitar ready. She knew what I needed. She nodded in rhythm, once, twice, three, and I smoothly came into the song.

Nice. Thank you, Stella.

If I'm honest, I don't really know what Stella's lyrics are about. She makes them sound oblique and obscure, and poetic. It sounds good. That's all I know.

By the time we were five songs in, we all felt like we had the audience in the palm of our hands.

Sometimes, some shows, you feel like you have to work the audience the whole time, just to get them to give a shit. Some shows, this show, they are there for you from the start.

It was work for me, though.

Every song, I just hoped I was coming in more or less right, and driving the beat similar to what IQ usually does.

GQ helped. Any time I felt at all unsure, I just locked onto whatever rhythm I got from his bass, and did my best to roll with it.

I'm sure there were a few songs I fucked up, but Stella, Andre, and GQ all seemed happy enough. Bottom line; it sounded good.

"Thanks," Stella said, after we wound down a song called "Random Bully."

Cheering and whistles.

"Thanks," she said again. "Some of you might have noticed we don't have our regular drummer tonight." She paused dramatically. "IQ, wherever you are out in the world tonight, be safe."

Then she turned and smiled at me. "I want to thank Zenny Zeller for sitting in tonight."

Surprisingly, a few people yelled, and not in a negative way.

"Zenny was the drummer for Gupper Fish back in the day."

More whoops. Some cheers.

I smiled and looked out at the crowd. I felt genuinely touched. No one should be cheering for me, but here were a handful of people who were doing just that. I tapped my fist to my heart and pointed at Stella. She smiled back at me, and turned back to the mic.

Then I looked down at the set list. We were about to get this crowd shakin' booty.

It was true, what I had told Allie the night before. I don't usually dance. I'm usually on drums when everybody else is dancing.

This would be one of those songs.

Another Notch Higher

The show seemed to have a spontaneous build to it. Maybe it wasn't completely spontaneous. Stella knew what she was doing when she wrote the set list.

The trick to putting together a good set list is knowing when you can get away with the slow song. Better yet, knowing when the slow song is exactly the right thing at the right time.

Stella has a song she does solo. No drums. No Andre. Just her voice, her guitar. I guess it's the one song I know all the lyrics to, because she sings it alone in the living room when she thinks no one's around.

I freely admit this right now, with you as my witness. I have a sentimental side, and that song gets me every time I hear it. Some female singers have a way of being something I can only call "feminine tough."

There is a toughness to their emotional songs that kills me.

The song was also a break for us three guys.

I wiped my face with my shirt sleeve. I was sweating. It had been a while since I'd done a whole live show. It was going well and all, but I was starting to feel like I'd been playing football for an hour.

I managed to catch my breath and relax. When Stella eased into the final notes of her solo song, the crowd erupted. She had touched them. It was an amazing feeling. This kind of intimacy - a medium-sized crown in a medium-sized club - is what famous bands miss when they play stadiums. There's no intimacy. Stella had all of us, myself included, in her celestial orbit.

I looked down at the set list, and tried to shake myself back to consciousness.

Andre kicked one of his foot pedals. The sound he gets from his guitar to start this next song can best be described as 'elegant feedback.'

He pounded out his power chord intro. I poured myself into my drum kit harder than I had all evening. GQ thumped a heart-pounding bass riff. Stella turned to her mic and took us all another notch higher.

Glazer From Polymorph

There are moments in music when the bond between musicians transcends friendship. It transcends love. It is something other. That's the best way I can describe it. It's something other.

I've played a lot of music in my time. I've played good shows and bad shows. With Gupper Fish we had a few that rocked at a pretty high level. I could count down my top five shows I'd played in.

Maybe it was the heat of the moment, but damn if I didn't tell myself this was the best damn show I'd been a part of in my whole life.

We did an encore song, and Stella told the crowd thanks and good night, and the four of us gathered in the cramped space to the side of the stage.

Stella hugged me and then hugged Andre and GQ. The crowd was still whistling and stomping.

Andre and I gave each other a quick hug, and GQ and I tapped each other on the back.

The crowd was still going wild.

We were not getting out of here tonight without going back out on that stage one more time.

"What do we have left?" Stella asked.

"I have something," Andre said.

He was looking at Stella intently. She looked back at him, and I felt the very distinct feeling that it was a song of Andre's that the two of them had argued about.

There was a brief frozen silence between them.

The crowd was getting louder.

"Okay," Stella said.

We followed Andre onto the stage.

I yelled up at him from behind, "What do you want from me, Andre?"

He turned around and said, "Just find the groove and do your thing, Zenny."

I smiled and sat at my drum kit.

"Thank you," Stella said looking out at the crowd. "Thanks so much."

The crowd was satisfied and happy. They quieted down a bit, but not completely. A few lingering cheers and whistles popped up here and there.

"This is called 'Quantum Soul,'" Andre said.

Really? I thought. Quantum Soul? Don't fuck this up, Andre.

But he kicked into a pretty rocking guitar riff. I waited for the right moment and jumped in with my sticks.

GQ found a simple but rocking bass line.

Stella stood to the side and just tried to back up Andre on rhythm guitar.

I don't have any idea what Andre was singing about. Probably some pretentious bullshit.

It didn't matter.

Andre was the only person who would ever know what that song was about.

It rocked just hard enough to keep the crowd happy, and when it was over they erupted into a spontaneous wave of happy noise.

We were off stage again, hugging each other again, and finally relaxing.

Since it wasn't much of a backstage, a few people from the crowd ran back to take pictures with us.

Then HE came backstage.

Glazer from Polymorph.

Glazer is an older guy, bald but stylish in sunglasses (even indoors and at night). He dressed in a sort of studied casual look. He appeared with two beautiful women, one on each side of him.

He strode confidently toward Stella, smiled a big broad smile, and put his arms out. "Beautiful," he said, wrapping Stella in a hug. "Absolutely beautiful."

"Thank you," Stella said. "Thanks so much."

"You're all brilliant," he said, mostly, I thought, to Andre.

Glazer and Stella stood facing each other. "You," he said. "You, I believe in. you're going to be a star. You have that special something."

Stella has never been great at taking over-the-top praise. She stammered awkwardly and said "thanks" again.

Then Glazer finally looked at me. "I like it," he said. "I like the laid back older drummer thing."

I thought about calling him out on which of us was actually older, but managed to hold my tongue.

"Well, thanks so much," Stella said. "Thanks for coming."

"Wouldn't have missed it, not for all the money in the world. Let's meet. Come to my office. When are you free? Can you come tomorrow?"

"Y - yes," Stella said. "We can come tomorrow."

One of the women was checking her phone and looked up. "Two O'clock?"

"T - two O'clock, we'll be there," Stella echoed.

Glazer looked at me again, and said, "You're going to forget you were ever in Gupper Fish."

"If I have enough to drink, I almost forget now," I said.

"Well." He reached his arms out to give Stella another hug. "Fantastic, fantastic, I'll see you tomorrow."

"Thanks again," Stella said

He shook Andre's hand and said, "Brilliant."

"Thanks."

He shook GQ's hand. "Rock solid."

GQ nodded.

He shook my hand and said, "And you're crazy but I love you."

"Good to know, man," I said.

Then Glazer from Polymorph turned and walked away, and the two beautiful women followed him.

Stella turned to me with her eyes wide open. "What just happened?"

I shrugged. "Don't assume anything just happened. Wait till tomorrow. I'm just glad he didn't use the word 'fabulous.' I might have thrown up on him if he did."

Chapter Eight

Selling cars

"What do you really think, Zenny? Is he for real?"

Stella was driving. I was in the passenger seat.

Our gear was loaded in behind me. GQ was sitting in his usual spot, silent, tiny speakers in his ears, staring out the window.

It was two in the morning.

Andre wasn't with us

Some girl, again.

There was an impromptu after party. The club spotted us our drinks, which I had a few too many of, while Stella had a few too few.

Now we were driving through the quiet middle of the L.A. night.

"He's gonna have some ideas," I said. "He's gonna suggest certain things, musical ideas, what's hot right now, what we should all fucking look like."

"He better not try to change us," Stella said.

"He'll try. My guess is he won't try to outright change us, just tweak us, smooth out our rough edges."

She looked over at me, and asked, "What are our rough edges? What do you think he doesn't like?"

"Hell, I don't know," I said. "I'm guessing. Maybe he'll really listen to us, and let us do whatever the fuck we want. I doubt it though."

"He better not try to change us," she said again.

"He's got money. That's the good news. If we don't fuck things up, if he's more or less rational, we'll get some of it. Save our asses. Save the fucking house."

Stella drove, her gaze burning through the windshield. "What's the worst thing?" she asked. "I want to be prepared for the worst thing he would want from us."

"The worst thing? I don't know. Maybe he'd try to sell your most personal song for a car ad. Ready for something like that? Your most personal song being used to sell cars?"

Stella didn't respond at first. She looked over toward me. "Would he really do that?"

"Well, you know, his job is to make money with our music."

"I'm going to have to think about that," she said.

"Remember the Bob Dylan Super Bowl ad?" I asked.

"Hm? No, what?"

"Bob Dylan did a huge Chrysler ad, Super Bowl ad. People asked, 'Why is Bob Dylan becoming a shill for Chrysler?' Not too many people noticed that the song in the ad had the line, 'I used to care, but things have changed.'"

She laughed.

We turned the corner, drove slowly down our familiar residential street, and turned into the driveway. It was dark, but something caught my eye. As Stella was turning off the engine, I stepped out and walked toward the front steps. Someone was sitting there in the dark.

I stepped closer.

"IQ," I said.

"Hi, Zenny."

He had shaved off his hair. He was wearing a white shawl wrapped around his body.

He was barefoot.

"IQ!" Stella shouted. "What the fuck!"

He stood up and faced us.

Several things went through my mind in a half-second.

First was the thought that my guest stint in the band was over. Too good to be true. My second thought was that IQ had lost his mind.

"Hey, man." GQ hardly flinched when he saw his brother.

Stella was beside herself. "Where have you been? What the fuck is going on?"

"I wanted to say good bye," IQ said.

"Good b - What the - "

"I've joined a Buddhist monastery. I'll be living there."

The silence that followed went on a lot longer than it should have.

"Hey," I said, "That's, that's cool. A monastery, huh. That's wild."

"Zenny, it's because of you. You inspired me."

"I inspired you?"

"Haven't you ever explored the meaning of your own name?"

"Sure, man, of course, but - "

"Why don't we all go inside and talk about it?" Stella suggested. "We have your wallet. You dropped it outside the club that night."

"I don't want my wallet," IQ said. "I don't want anything." Then he turned to his brother. "Tell Mom and Dad I love them. They can come visit me any time."

GQ nodded casually.

"What is happening?" Stella asked no one in particular.

"How exactly does this relate to me?" I asked.

"You're a Shaman," he said.

"A Sham- that's not even Buddhist, is it. That's Native American. That's fire dancing, or something. I'm no Shaman."

IQ looked from me to Stella. "I don't think I can explain this," he said. "Maybe it's better if I don't try. What I know is that I don't want all this striving, all this empty ambition."

"This is fucking nuts," Stella said.

IQ looked intently at Stella. "I don't expect you to understand this now. You've taught me, Stella. You've taught me a lot."

We all stood awkwardly, looking at the ground.

"Goodbye," he said, and he walked across the grass toward the street with his bare feet.

"IQ," I yelled, "where are you going?"

"To the monastery," he yelled back.

"Where's that?"

"Eleven miles."

"Let us drive you."

"No thanks."

And he was gone.

Stella looked from me to GQ and back.

None of us knew what to say.

Finally I reached into my pocket for the keys and unlocked the front door of the house.

We turned on the lights.

I sat on the couch. Stella sat across from me. GQ went into the kitchen and came back with an open box of cereal. He reached his hand in and shoved the handful of dry cereal into his mouth.

Stella's gaze locked in on GQ.

"You knew," she said.

He shook his head, casually swallowing his mouthful of cereal. "Not really," he said.

"Come on, GQ."

He took a breath and sighed. "He said he was thinking about some things. He was dabbling in Buddhism again. He never said he was going to live in a monastery."

"But the whole time, you were never worried about him."

"Yes, I was."

"It was because of me," Stella said.

"Maybe a little."

Stella looked at me.

I shrugged. "Hey," I said, "being in love with you is a helluva thing."

She sighed and smiled.

"Oh god," she said, "and I almost forgot we have an appointment with Glazer tomorrow."

"We sure do," I said.

"I hope Andre fucking makes it," she said.

"He'll be there," I assured her.

She smiled a tired smile. Then she dropped her arms and let out a long sigh.

Suddenly the weight of the entire last two days permeated the room.

"My head hurts," Stella said. "I need a beer."

She stood up and wandered toward the kitchen. "Anyone else?"

"Yes," I said.

"Sure," said GQ.

I listened to her rummage around in the kitchen. GQ's eyes met mine.

"You thinking of following him?" I asked.

"Hm?"

"Your brother. Live in the monastery."

"No, fuck that. I want to be a fucking rock star."

He said it just as Stella returned with the three beers. "Me too," she said. "How about you Zenny?"

I shrugged. "Sure, I guess so."

"You guess so!?"

"Someone once told me that no matter how hard you try to get away from the shitty things in life, the one person you can never get away from is yourself. Being famous doesn't solve your problems. You still have to deal with yourself. You never stop being a human being."

"What are you saying?" Stella handed us each our beers. "Is IQ right?"

"He's right and he's wrong. He's right and he's left. He's ipso facto undeniably deniable. We're right too. Stella, as long as you're expressing your gut, honestly, there ain't nothin' wrong with being a rock star."

"Shit, Zenny, I don't know if you're making shit up, or giving me the universal secret."

"The secret is, there's no secret."

"Shut up," Stella said playfully.

She sat on the couch next to me, pulled her feet up underneath her, and leaned against me. She laid her head on my shoulder, took a sideways swig from her beer, and said, "This should be the happiest day of my life, but all I am is tired,"

Chapter Nine

That night I had a dream.

I dreamed about IQ walking barefoot across Los Angeles.

I dreamed that is bare feet felt good walking across eleven miles of pavement.

His face had a look of peacefulness as he walked. At times his eyes were open. At times they were closed.

Sometimes he would inhale a deep breath, eyes closed, then exhale, letting all his troubles out with the breath, open his eyes, and relax.

Always walking, but with a calm look on his face.

Walking and walking.

And then my dream went into the future, and he was still a monk, but he was beginning to question it.

I dreamed he was sitting in a chair outside, at the top of a hill, looking off into the valley below, staring at everything and nothing.

Then I dreamed that he stood up from his outdoo⁻ chair and walked away. This time, though, he walked away from being a Buddhist monk.

The guy who had walked away from everything ir his life, was now also walking away from this.

Then I began to dream about Stella.

I dreamed that we were in Glazer's office, signing papers. We were all smiling. Glazer was smiling. Stella was smiling. Andre was smiling. I was smiling. GQ, well, he never smiles, but he was in a good mood anyway.

Then I dreamed we were playing a show, in a big arena, and even though we missed the intimacy of the small club, Stella still held the audience in the palm of her hand, intimately, and the audience loved her for it.

Then I dreamed that it was after the show, and groupies came back stage, male and female, all of them wanting to be around Stella.

She was nice to all of them, because she genuinely appreciated them.

Then I dreamed that some of the beautiful girls began to flock around Andre, and he loved it. He soaked up the attention. Then I dreamed that GQ was talking to a single girl from the crowd, and she followed him, and they disappeared down a hallway.

Then I dreamed that a crazy girl came up to me. She had lipstick all over her face, and a big mouth, and lots of crooked pointy teeth, and when she laughed her face came apart, and I screamed.

I ran. I ran and ran, but I was running on nothing, no ground, just air, but I kept running.

And then I was falling.

But in my dream, my fall began to slow down.

I was falling slower and slower, until I touched down gently on the grass in front of my house.

I walked to the front door and opened it, and I felt relieved because the house was still there and I still lived in it.

And then my dream went into the future.

I was older, but still sitting at my drums, and in front of me was Stella.

She was older too, but not as old as me.

Andre wasn't there in my dream. We had some other guitarist, who I didn't recognize, but he was good.

And there was GQ, older but the same.

And we were playing a show as the older band, playing a song that the audience loved, because it had been Stella's big hit song years ago – but still in the future from the moment I was dreaming it.

And I dreamed that the audience knew all the words and were singing along.

And I dreamed that it was after the show, but there was a lot less sexual craziness backstage.

The people from the audience who made it backstage were calm but happy, and they genuinely loved Stella because she had made music that was a part of their lives. And Stella still genuinely appreciated all of them.

And then I dreamed that she came over to me and sat next to me and put her arm around me and kissed me.

And then I dreamed that our twelve-year-old son ran up, and then our ten-year-old daughter.

I dreamed that they were good kids, intelligent and creative, except that they liked to do whatever they weren't supposed to do, like all kids.

And I dreamed that Stella and I looked each other in the eyes and kissed each other.

And then I woke up from the dream.

I was in my same bed, in my same room. The sun was shining in through the curtain.

I just lay in bed without moving, looking up at the ceiling.

It was a good dream. I liked it. I felt good.

It was the first time I had finished a dream in days.

So I just kept lying there without moving.

And I knew the dream would not quite come true the way I dreamed it.

We would sign the papers with Glazer. We would play the shows. The audience years from now would sing along to their favorite song. But Stella and I would not be together, and we would not have kids.

And that's okay.

I can have my dream. Being in love with Stella is a helluva thing.

The real me and the real Stella will always love each other in a different way.

Then I heard voices in the living room. Stella, GQ, Andre.

I sat slowly up on the edge of the bed.

I didn't move for a few minutes.

I closed my eyes and breathed.

Life is good, I told myself.

Then I stood up and opened the bedroom door. I walked toward the kitchen, and saw Andre sitting on the couch.

I opened the fridge and searched for a couple of cheese sticks. I found them, and turned to walk to the living room.

As I walked around the couch Stella smiled at me from her usual chair.

GQ was standing, shoving another handful of cereal into his mouth.

I sat down on the couch near Andre.

"What time is it? When's our meeting?" I asked.

"We should leave in about an hour," Stella said.

I bit off a piece of cheese and looked over at Andre.

"How's it going?" I asked.

"Everything's good," he said.

I looked across at Stella.

"How about you?"

Her smile widened.

"I'm pretty fucking happy," she said. "How about you, Zenny? Are you ready to become a rock star again?"

I thought for a moment before answering. "I've never been a rock star," I said. "I'm the drummer. People take the drummer for granted. But, you know, that's okay. It is what it is, you know. It is what it fucking is."

Then Stella turned to GQ.

"Fuck, GQ, say something."

He moved his hand to his mouth and chomped down on a mouthful of cereal. He chewed slowly, looking from one of us to the other. "What Zenny said," he said, chewing some more. "What Zenny said."

About The Author:

Peter Wick is an award-winning independent filmmaker and writer. He has Produced, Written, Directed, and Acted in three independent feature films, all with the support of grants from Seattle non-profit, Northwest Film Forum. All three films have won film festival awards. Most recently Peter won "Best Director" at the New York International Film Festival in 2011, for his feature, "Rock Paper Scissors." He has also performed stand-up comedy at clubs around the United States. His first novel was "Key West," set in the rough and tumble world of 1950 Florida politics. He currently lives in Los Angeles, California.

Follow Peter Wick on Twitter: @juventinopw
Visit his website: www.Peter-Wick.com

Peter Wick's films

Rock Paper Scissors won Wick the Best Director Award at the New York International Film Festival in 2011. It tells the story of Marty (Wick), the ex-basketball star turned PE teacher, and Lana, his long ago high school sweetheart, now the eccentric high school science teacher (former "Miss Italy" Roberta Orlandi). When they meet, years after their original affair, old passions re-ignite. But she's married, he's not. Romance, passion, and humor combine to tell a very human story.

Available on Amazon

Movie Pizza Love won the Indiefest's Feature Film Award-of-merit in 2008, as well the Original Song award for co-star Jen Casebeer's song, "Trashy Novel." The ultimate low budget film, Wick made this award-winning feature with a total budget of just $5,000, shooting over three weeks with a volunteer crew.

"Art" (Wick) is making a film about his singer-songwriter friend Lisa (Casebeer). The movie-within-a-movie (within-a-movie) twists in on itself, as Art slowly realizes the friend is more important than the movie. Funny, thoughtful, and unpredictable, this film has been included on more than 100 'favorite films' lists around the world.

Available on Amazon

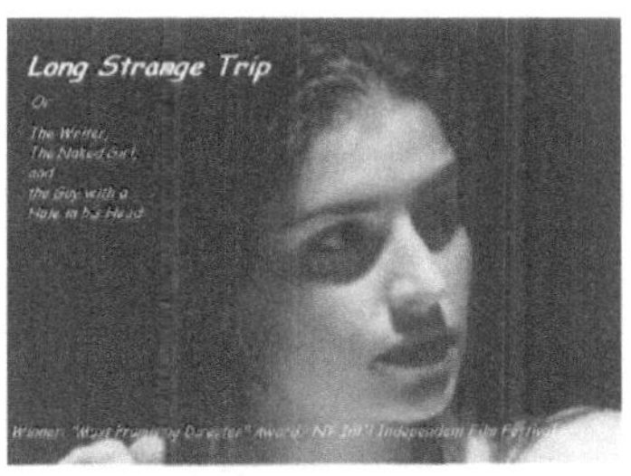

Long Strange Trip, Wick's debut feature, won him the "Most Promising Director" award at 1999's NYIIFVF. The film follows "Phil" (Wick) on a bizarre, twisted descent into absurdity, billed as a 'comic homage' to "Apocalypse Now." After losing his magazine column, his book deal, and his relationship with his Editor/girlfriend Andrea, Phil is assigned to interview a stripper. When the stripper's brother Lars enters the story, sporting a festering bullet wound to the head, all sanity is lost. Included on several lists of longest movie titles of all time, the full title of the film is, "Long Strange Trip – or The Writer, The Naked Girl, and The Guy with a hole in his Head."

Available at Indieflix.com

www.Peter-Wick.com

Twitter: @juventinopw
Blog: www.PeterWick.blogspot.com
YouTube: Azzurri Productions

Peter Wick's books

Key West – Special Edition (2015) combines Wick's original 2013 novel
with prequel short story, "The King of the Keys." Inspired by real events,
Key West chronicles the 1950's battle between corrupt Florida state
representative Bernie Papy, and 'hardboiled' journalist, Miami Herald
columnist Stephen Trumbull. Mark Howell of the Key West Citizen called
Wick's novel, "An engaging, fun read," and one Amazon customer review
raved "[I] cannot put it down."

Key West – The Companion Episodes (2015) brings Wick's original 2013
and 2014 follow-up episodes (originally published by Wheelman Press as
kindle-only novellas) together under one cover for the first time. It is 1951
and Florida state representative Bernie Papy is pulling all the strings.
Trumbull is using his Miami Herald column to expose Papy. "The
Companion Episodes" tells a gripping story of danger, corruption,
backroom deals, and Trumbull's relentless search for the truth.

It is **W**hat it **I**s

a novella

Peter Wick

It Is What It Is (2015) Seventeen years ago Zenny Zeller was the drummer of one-hit wonder band "Gupper Fish." Now he rents space in his house to the beautiful Stella and her band. Stella's drummer, I.Q., has disappeared....again. Zenny and the band bumble through one possible lead after another, hoping to find I.Q. before their big club show for industry mogul, Glazer-from-Polymorph. Along the way they encounter an endless parade of colorful characters, some of them burned out old friends of Zenny's from "back in the day." This new light hearted novella from Wick humorously weaves a fun and funny tale, inspired in part by Wick's own history on the fringes of the "grunge" music scene.